HARRISON AMBUSH BOOK 5

KATHI S. BARTON

World Castle Publishing, LLC
Pensacola, Florida
Copyright © Kath S. Barton
Paperback ISBN: 9781629896991
eBook ISBN: 9781629897004
First Edition World Castle Publishing, LLC, May 15, 2017
http://www.worldcastlepublishing.com

Cover: Karen Fuller
Editor: Maxine Bringenberg

Chapter 1

Liam loved the house. He walked through it once more, just to be sure he wasn't feeling something that wasn't there. Nope, he thought to himself, he loved this place. Trying hard not to show how much he did, he walked around the big empty living room once more to calm himself and his inner cat. There wasn't any point in giving away his happiness before making an offer.

"This room alone is nearly as big as the house that I live in." The realtor smiled at him. "What do you think, Mr. Harrison…is this a place you can put down roots?"

"I'm not sure." He thought he sounded like he was bored and had to take a deep breath before continuing. "The kitchen needs to be redone. I mean, from the studs. There are going to be issues with the furnace, as well as the air conditioning before too much longer. Also, I think I saw rat droppings in the garage."

Which he knew wouldn't be a problem once he moved in. He'd bet by now there wasn't one within ten miles of the place. Him being a tiger tended to take care of that sort of thing. He asked her what the selling price was again, knowing full well what it was.

"The house hasn't been lived in for about four months…I

believe that's the time frame. And before that, I do believe that they had the place exterminated. *If* you're seeing droppings, I'm not sure where they came from. But the bank is very motivated to sell. They're asking four hundred, but I think I can get them to go a little lower, but not too much. I do know that the house needs work. Like I said, it's been empty for a few months while things were settled." Liam nodded. He knew just exactly why it had been sitting, and that it had been a good deal longer than a few months. "I can go in at a lower price, but I believe they have multiple offers so I'd not expect too much."

"All right then. Thank you for your time." She shook his hand when it was offered and Liam made his way to the door.

"Wait. I don't understand. Did you want me to make an offer?" He told her no. "No? I thought you were interested in this house."

"I am, but not at four hundred thousand dollars. As I said, it needs a great deal of work. And there are no other offers on the table, I know that as well as you do. I also did my research on this place, and I know the real reason that it's sat here for the last seventeen years. The previous owner had paid up the taxes for the last fifteen years and there wasn't anything you could do about it until recently. Four hundred thousand is well over fair market, and double what the house was selling for last year when your firm took over for the bank in trying to sell it." He moved toward the door again and turned as he opened the door. "I'll just wait and get it from the bank next month when it goes up for auction. Thanks anyway."

Liam was out the door before she could find her tongue. But that didn't stop her from following him and yelling out a lower price. He thought that three hundred was too much as well, and got into his truck and left. He wanted the house, but he wanted it on his terms.

Are you done with the house? He told Storm that he was. *Good. I think you should stop by our house. There is a large vehicle, and that's an understatement, in the drive, and the person in it is asking for you. Not nicely, I might add. Hudson is her name.*

Why is she...? You know what, I don't care. She's the woman that I was telling you about on the deal with Whites. She said she had some information on her father maybe picking up the loads that they're missing. Any luck finding Mr. Hudson, by the way? Storm told him she was still looking. *He really fucked her over.*

Not the only one either, from what I've been able to find out. But he did royally fuck her over with her job. She had a good rep, as you said, and he's really taken her for a ride. Lost her house, car, as well as her savings trying to keep herself out of jail. I'd like to find this fucker myself. Liam said that he would as well. *She's currently at her truck, walking around it. I don't know why, but I kind of think that she's had enough of the open road for a while. She looks beaten.*

Liam made a left to go to his brother's home, and smiled when he thought of the temper of the woman, Hudson. When he'd spoken to her last night—well, earlier that morning—he'd been sleep confused, but hearing her voice and what she had to say had him getting up and going back to his computer. He was going to find her father if he had to do it on his own.

The rig was parked in the long drive to his brother's house. The woman was circling the back end, the place where the big trailer was attached. He watched her for several minutes as she moved around it like a little monkey, checking the lines and lights as she went. When she jumped down, she stared at him as he did her. Christ, she was beautiful.

"Liam?" He nodded at her question. "I was close enough to bring them to you, and I'm not so trusting of the postal service on something like this. I need them back, so you know. I might need them should Daddy dearest come back for some more of my ass."

"He won't." Liam had no idea why he said that. He didn't know either of them. But as she made her way to the front of her truck and climbed in, he made his way there, with Riordan and Storm coming with him. "She's got his log books, but she needs them back."

"She should put them in a safe. If he knows she has them, he'll come for them." Liam wasn't sure he'd not already tried and told Riordan that. "Watch her."

Hudson came tumbling back and he leapt to catch her. He had no idea what had taken her down, but as he caught her in his arms, two things occurred to him. One, she was bleeding, and the second thing was that she was his mate.

"Christ, that fucking hurt." He held her for as long as she allowed him to, then set her down on her feet. "I've been meaning to have that fixed. Fuck, that hurt."

"Let me see. I've called Ennis, he's on his way." Liam wasn't a doctor, but he knew this wound looked bad. Not just bad, but there was a lot of blood streaming from it. Liam wanted to lick it, to taste her, but he was afraid to. She looked like she could take him on and come out on top. "It's going to need some stitches, as well as cleaned up. When was your last tetanus shot?"

"Last year. I cut myself on the same fucking place on my other hand. Stupid of me for not getting it fixed then." He looked at her wrist and saw the long scar. It went from her elbow to her palm. This one wasn't quite that long, but it was deep. "I don't feel so well."

"You're cut deep. I have to heal you." He heard Riordan caution him, but he was losing her and had to do something.

8

As soon as she fainted, he shifted. The roaring in his head was making him sick. They were losing their mate and neither of them were happy about it.

His cat whimpered but knew what to do. As soon as he licked the wound closed, tasting her blood as he did so, he seemed to realize at the same moment that she was too weak, that they'd waited too long. Growling at the couple that were too close to them, his cat bit deeply into her belly, tearing it open as he did so.

"Hurry, Liam. You're going to lose her if you don't." He knew that and snarled at Storm, making her laugh. "Just trying to help. I'm assuming that she's your mate."

Yes, and I don't want to hear you making fun of me just yet. He was pissy and wasn't sure why, but he bit into her leg. Holding his mouth deep in the wound, he looked up at his brother. Riordan was afraid for him, and Liam didn't feel any better about this. *I have a feeling she's not going to be thrilled when she wakes and finds out what I've done.*

"More than likely not. But it was that or she was dead. I can hear her heart picking up, can you?" He told him he could. "Just a few more minutes now and you should be able to release her. I'll take her inside and put her in the bedroom that you use when here."

Thank you. Riordan nodded and called to someone on the porch to bring out some blankets. *Riordan, she's got some pretty horrific memories in here. Mostly about her father. He took her for everything, forcing her to live in this truck.*

"I know. I read the report Stormy found. When you release her, go in the house and shower and change. Once you are settled, I'll bring you what we've been able to find out. Also, Marcy Cochran called about the house. She wants you to make a reasonable offer."

9

Liam let the young woman go, but he wasn't ready to leave her yet. Her heartrate had picked up and he could see the wound at her wrist was nearly healed, as were the ones he'd given her. It had been a big chance, doing this with her blood flowing so quickly, but he couldn't let her die no matter what kind of mood she was going to be in when she found out.

Riordan picked her up and carried her into the house, and he followed. When she was on the bed, her skin warmer now that she was a cat, he left her to Stormy, who said she'd clean her up for him.

Going into the bathroom, he looked in the mirror after becoming a man again and stared at the person there. He had a mate. And there was a very good chance that she was going to kill him when she found out. Smiling, Liam reached into the stall and turned the water on. Christ, he was way too happy, he thought, for someone that had just converted a person without their knowledge.

By the time he was dressed and sitting in the chair beside her, he'd figured out a few things. She wasn't happy with what she did as a driver, mostly because she had no relief from it. Also, her father had hurt more than her finances when he ran off. She hadn't trusted him, not entirely, but the fact that he'd taken advantage of her so profoundly had nearly taken her under.

He looked up when Stormy came in the room with a file.

"The courts went by the books on this. There is no fault according to them. She had to sell her house as well as her car, which wasn't a new one but all she had, when the trucking dealership wanted all their money. The truck is still missing, it appears." He asked if her father had it. "I'm thinking not. I don't know why, but I think he sold it for the money, and someone else is driving it that knows about trackers and such. Might be wrong, but I think that's it. We have the LoJack information, and since we can't find it that way, we've come to the conclusion that it's been taken out. Also, you know it is against the law."

If she thought that, then it was more than likely true. "I told Ennis not to worry about rushing now. I told him what happened, but not that she is my mate."

"He knows. So do your parents." He asked her how that had happened. "Riordan was covered in blood when they showed up, Hudson's blood, and your mom sort of freaked out. He had to tell them."

"I guess. I'm trying to figure out what to tell her when she wakes up." The woman on the bed stirred and he watched, sure that she was going to wake a great deal sooner than anyone would have expected. "I have to help her out, with all of this."

"Liam, can I ask you a personal question?" He just looked at her. "Okay, some of it I know, like where you have a portion of your money invested. How much the books say you're worth. But what is it you do? I mean, I know you work for the family business when they need you, but that can't be all that you do, is it?"

"I'm a businessman." She snorted at him. "Okay, I'm a very good businessman. I invest low and sell high. For everything. I'm good at bargaining on things as well. Like the house. I'm going to get it, but not at the asking price. Then, if Emma doesn't care for it, I'll sell it for a great deal more than I purchased it for."

"Why would me liking your house have anything to do with whether or not you sell it?" He grinned and said hi to her. "It's Hudson. No one calls me by my first name."

She lifted her arm and looked at it. There wasn't a wound anymore, and no scars on the rest of her body. He'd not seen her yet, her body, but he'd bet that it was lovely. He started to tell her, just talk to her gently about it, but Stormy laughed before speaking.

"You were dying. The cut to your wrist had severed your artery, and you were bleeding out. Had Liam not been here for you, you'd be dead." Emma asked him what he'd done, but Stormy continued. "He's a shifter, Bengal tiger as a matter of fact. We all are. He converted you to what we are."

Emma stared at him for several seconds, then looked over at Storm. There was a lot going on in her head right now. None of it very nice, nor all that orderly. She went from terror of her dying to being converted. He was just glad that she knew enough about paranormals to have an idea of what was happening.

"I'm a tiger." Storm nodded. "And you thought that my being a tiger was a better way to go than to be dead?"

"Yes, I did." She turned and looked at him. "You're not freaking out, so I can only assume that you know about our kind."

"I do. I don't have a lot of contact with them...not because I avoid them, but.... You did this because we're mates. You saved me because of some kind of DNA thing that makes you have to save me." He said that he would have anyway. "No, you wouldn't have. Don't lie to me."

"I can't." She nodded and sat up, but he could see that she was slightly dizzy. "You lost a great deal of blood, so you might want to take it easy for a few hours. You should try and drink a lot and have a light—"

"Don't order me around." He leaned back in the chair and looked at her. "I'm not.... I know you really didn't, but I'm starting to freak a little here. I'm a fucking tiger."

~~~

Hudson lay on the bed thinking about her life and what had just happened. "I don't know what I'm supposed to do."

"Me either." She turned to her back and looked at him. "I'm not going to apologize for converting you. I could, I guess, but you're alive, and that's the most important thing right now. I don't know anything about you other than what I've read in the information that Storm got for us when you called me. And you know even less than that about me. What would you like to know? If anything."

"What was your name again?" He told her. "All right, Liam. I'm Emma Hudson, but I rarely go by my first name. I have no idea why, but that's what they started calling me in middle school and that stuck. I drive cross country. Not as much as I used to, but sometimes I need the money more than I do anything. I had a home, but I had to sell it to pay for the rig that my father stole. Which he did, no matter what the courts say."

"Storm, my sister-in-law—and so you know, you met her when you came here—she doesn't think he has it anymore." She nodded, thinking that Storm had some good connections. "Your load you have now, you mentioned that it was a back run. Does that have to go out today?"

"Not today, but soon. I have to have it about six hours from here by noon tomorrow." He leaned back in his chair. "What about me being a cat? I mean, I can sort of feel something inside of me. What does that mean?"

"She's letting you know that she's there for you. I can sense that you're nervous, and so can she." Hudson sat up but lay back down when her head spun. "You're going to be a little weak for a few more hours, like I said. Ennis, he's my brother and a doctor, he said that if you were to eat something hearty, you'd feel a lot better. But he wanted you to eat it slowly, in case it doesn't stay down well."

"I've not had a home cooked meal in years." She laughed.

13

"I'm sorry. That was rude of me. But the thought of something not mass produced or from a microwave sounds amazing."

"I think we can fix you up." He stood up and his size made her recoil. "I'd never hurt you. Not on purpose, if I can help it."

"My dad, he's a big man. Not that he ever hit me, but he was cruel in other ways." He nodded and put out his hand. Hudson stared at it as she continued. "I know a few shifters, and I've heard that their mates are the center of their world. Also, that the sex is amazing and they can never harm them. They told me that any female, human or otherwise, is to be protected and cherished."

"Yes. We feel that way as well. I'd very much like it if you were to go with me to the house that I'm thinking of buying. If it doesn't suit you, then that's fine as well. I have a place that I live in, it's an apartment, if you'll come stay with me for a time." He cursed and she laughed. "There's this big deal of a wedding next weekend. My brother, Aedan, is getting married. They've been living together for a little while, but this wedding is going to be epic, I guess."

"Why?" He told her how he was the governor of the state and that he was looking into becoming the president someday. "Wow. Your family, they have big plans."

"They do. We all do." She nodded. "What is bothering you, Emma? Is it something that I can fix? Or do for you?"

"I'm assuming that you all have money." He nodded, but didn't say how much, which she thought was a good thing. "My father will get wind of this. Not that I'm a cat, but that I'm with someone with money, and he'll come sniffing around. He's not stupid, but he can play a person and get what he wants. No matter the cost to them."

"He can do that if he wants, but he won't get away with it this time. I can promise you that. Nor will he hurt you, mentally, physically, or financially." Hudson wasn't sure, but she was almost afraid for her dad. "Will you take my hand? Please?"

"What will that mean for us?" He said that it would only be him taking her to the kitchen for food for now. "I feel something for you. I'm not sure what it is, but I trust you. I want to be with you. Is that the cat in me?"

"Yes, for now anyway. I hope that later, you as a woman will feel something for me as well. We mate for life, and quickly." She still wasn't sure about this, none of it. "I want to take this slowly. I think it would benefit us both if we started out fresh, like we're dating. I know that we've gone beyond that, with me converting you and having this connection, but even my cat is okay with us doing it this way."

"I'm afraid." He said that he was as well. "What if he comes here? What if my dad comes here and makes demands? He will. I know it."

"How about we don't borrow trouble for now? We don't have to think about him until he gets here. And once we know where he is, we can keep an eye on his movements and be ready when it looks as if he's coming here." She nodded and put her hand in his. "Thank you. And for now, I think we should go and have ourselves a nice lunch, then get you ready to go on your trip. I'd like to go with you, but I won't be able to this trip. I have some things that are going on that need my attention."

"I thought we were going to be inseparable." They moved to the door, but he kept his arm around her when she was dizzy again. "I feel weird."

"Your cat again, and the loss of blood. Anyway, we usually are, inseparable I mean. But with us trying to work things out, I think that I'll not want to hunt you down every two minutes and strip you naked." She looked at him, trying her best to see if he was joking or not. When he laughed, Hudson still wasn't sure. But the smells coming from the kitchen had her thinking food rather than jokes.

As soon as she sat down with both Storm and Riordan, a platter, not a plate, of food was put in front of her. Hudson thought that she would never eat it all, but once she tasted the first bite, she knew that she'd be lucky if she didn't eat the platter too.

There was a thick roast beef sandwich on a wonderfully fresh roll with lettuce, tomatoes, pickles, and onions. A bowl of french fries covered in a tomato sauce that was spicy as well as sweet. A large glass of the best tea that she'd ever drank. She was just finishing off the last fry when June, the cook, asked her if she wanted peach or cherry pie. Hudson nodded.

"Well, good for you. I have ice cream too should you want that. I've not been to the creamery yet, so it won't be homemade." Hudson told her that she loved her. "Thank you, child. I'm so glad to be cooking for the household again. The mister and missus have been away more than at home of late, and I've missed it."

"You can cook for me whenever I'm home." Her face heated up. "I'm sorry. I don't know where I'm going to be living or what the plan is. But this is the best meal I've had in ages. And fresh pie too? Well, I could easily kiss you for it."

After she ate both pieces of pie without the ice cream—she didn't want to seem too piggish—her and Liam went to her truck. It was locked up, but as soon as she opened the door, she could see that someone had cleaned up after her. She asked Liam about it.

"I had a friend of mine come over and fix the bent metal. He also put a new handle on for you. Then his wife—she's the new alpha bitch for the wolf pack that roams our land—she cleaned up the rest for you. I think she was quite impressed with how much storage you have in there." She told Liam it was necessary when she was gone. "I don't imagine that it helped that you lost your house."

"He took me for a great many things. But my house was the most painful." Climbing into the truck, she watched him walk around to the other side and get in. He commented on how roomy it was. "Yes. My dad complained a great deal about how crowded it was for him. And you're much bigger. But he would have complained about it even if it had his recliner and a big screen television in front of him."

She showed him around the compartment that she had lived in. The way she had to pull her bed down to use it. There wasn't a lot of room when he was in it with her. For one, he was taller than her by a foot, and he was just too close. Or, she thought, not close enough. There was something extremely appealing about having this man near enough for her to not only touch, but to know that she could. Hudson thought maybe she was going insane.

Chapter 2

The bank manager was walking with them as they circled around the lower level again. The kitchen, Emma and he agreed, needed some extensive work. Not just the appliances, which had to have been purchased in the late sixties or early seventies, but also the counters, which looked like they had been covered with the same linoleum as the floor. Emma opened one of the cabinets, then turned to look at the banker.

"This place has mice." Winslow nodded and told her that it had been sitting empty for more than a decade. "Really? Because when Liam was with the realtor before, she made it sound as if it hadn't been that long ago that someone was here. A few months, didn't she say?"

"Four, and she said that the asking price is well over what you told me today. I'm not going to pay that much for a house that's been sitting for nearly twenty years. I'm sure that you wouldn't either." Liam winked at her when he turned to Winslow and continued. "Two hundred thousand is entirely too much to pay for this place. And the price she quoted me of four hundred grand is just is just ridiculous."

"Four hundred…. The price of this place was never that high. My goodness, Liam. Are you sure you heard her correctly?" He handed him the flyer that he'd picked up when she'd showed him around the other day. "I don't know what to say. I mean, if she's been doing this to.... We've had a few people in the last few months seem very excited about the house, but none of them ever...I'm thinking that this is more than likely why. Just horrible. You can bet that I'll be calling her boss as soon as I return to the bank. Liam, you know me, it's not the way I do business."

"I know that, Winslow. It's why I wanted to meet you here with my future wife. But I will make an offer. It won't be nearly as much as even you were asking, but I will promise you that I'll go through your bank to secure the loan if you can accept my offer."

"You tell me what it is and we'll work from there." He told him he'd give him seventy-five thousand for the house. "That's considerably less than I was hoping. But you're a good man, and I know your mom and dad well enough to know that if I don't accept this — which I can see is a reasonable offer now that I've walked around this place — they'll hound me to death at the next committee meeting."

"You know that I will do this place up right. Better than it had been." Winslow said he knew that about him too. "Thank you."

When they shook on the deal, Winslow said he'd have the paperwork ready when he returned to the bank. Liam waited until Winslow was out of sight in his little car before picking up Emma and swinging her around. This was going to be their home.

"This is going to take a lot of work. I mean, even just the little bit that you pointed out to him, I think it's going to be months before its even in a reasonable living condition." He told her that he knew that, but he had a plan. "I thought you might. But I do draw the line at both of us living in my truck for the next several months. There is barely enough room for me in that thing. You'd take up all the space."

"Before I forget, I've cleared my calendar, and if you'd allow it, I'd love to go with you on this trip. It'll keep me from getting on the contractor's nerves." He could tell that she was worried about that, and he was too a little. "We can get to know each other, and have some fun as well. I promise to be on my best behavior."

"You know, that isn't as comforting as you might think." He asked her why not. "Well, my idea of you at your best could be, and more than likely is, not the same as yours. I'm thinking that you're charming enough as it is. If you try and be more so, I might not survive a trip with you."

"I assure you, I'm a great deal of fun when you get to know me." He heard her mumble under her breath that was what scared her, but he only grinned. "When do we leave?"

"I have to be gone from here by midnight, sooner if I can manage it. When I have time, I like to drive four, rest four. It makes for easier driving, and plenty of time if something happens along the way. If you're going, you'll need to pack a few things. And we'll need to get some food for the trip. Speaking of which, your mom and dad invited us over for dinner." He knew that. The entire clan was going to be there. "Also, I've called my Aunt Eunice, Eunice Clarke—she's my dad's sister—and asked her about my dad, and I told her that you and I had.... She knows that you had to change me and why. She wants to meet you too. All of your family."

"Is she like your dad?" She told him she wasn't like anyone he'd ever met before. "I'm to take that as a no. So, she's like you. I can't wait to meet her."

"Yeah, you say that now, but once you do, there is no going

back from it. She's.... My Aunt Eunice rides a motorcycle, goes climbing, and takes a trip to Vegas once a year to show them how old people are supposed to behave. And that is not in a good way. She's what my friend who retired from driving used to call a pistol loaded with shot. My Uncle Alex, he passed on just after they were married, was killed in a shooting accident that my father was involved in. She's been filling her time getting into trouble since. Her words, not mine. She should be here in the next couple days."

"She sounds a great deal like you." Liam saw her face heat up and had to hide a smile. He wondered if she knew how much she envied her aunt. "I'll talk to Nikki and let her know that she'll be at the wedding too. I cannot wait to meet her."

"Aunt Eunice doesn't have to go." He asked her why not. "Because she'll be herself. And while I love her to death, she can be quite opinionated, as well as loud. Aunt Eunice does not know the meaning of whispering. Not when at the top of her lungs works so much better."

Liam thought she'd fit right in with his family. Speaking to Nikki about the aunt, he was told that Nikki wanted to have Hudson in the wedding too. He told her she was on her own with that one.

Yeah, I figured you'd say that. This will be perfect, she'll do it. If not, then I'll tell Stormy to talk to her. That'll make her do it. It would me. Liam wasn't sure that was going to work either. He had a feeling that Emma could hold her own with all four of his sisters-in-law. *Anyway. I'll talk to her tonight. You are still coming for dinner, right?*

Yes, but we're going to leave tonight. She has a delivery to do, and I want to get to know her. Nikki asked him if he was going to carry a gun. *I was planning on it. Why do you ask?*

Her dad. I've been.... Let me tell you both about what I've found out when you get here. Also, we're going to take pictures of the two of you tonight while you're here to put in the paper. It's necessary to draw the bastard out of hiding. Liam told her what Emma had told him. *Yes, she's correct in thinking that. He's been a very naughty boy, and we're going to hang his ass out to dry.*

That sounded sort of scary. *I'm going to make a couple of calls about the house. I got it, by the way, and for a good deal less than the asking. While we're gone, I'm going to have some of the work started.* She told him she was leaving for their honeymoon soon so wouldn't be able to do much. *It's all right. I'm going to use the vets that Stormy does. I like helping them out as much as they do me.*

Good idea. Okay, I should get going here. I have lots to do before this big deal goes on. Whoever thought it would be a great idea to have this enormous wedding needs to come and have a conversation with me. Christ, who knew the shit that had to be taken care of? He told her that he loved her. *I love you too, Liam. And take care of your mate. She's going to need it, I'm afraid.*

Lima drove them to the new offices of the Vet Construction Company. Stormy had set it up for them a few months ago, and business was booming. Liam did like using these gentlemen, and had never had any troubles with them. When he told Emma what he was going to do, she was all for it. They entered the offices and asked to speak to Big Ben. He had no idea why he was called that, the man was as skinny as a nail. But he was in charge.

~~~

Ordan watched the newest addition to his family. She was a pretty little thing. Not as tall as the other women he'd adopted as his own, but she was just as feisty. He loved that most about his new daughters, he thought with a grin. And right now, Stormy was about to get her ass handed to her if the look on Hudson's face was any indication.

23

"You need to carry a gun while he's out there." Hudson said no and picked up her fork to eat. "I don't want you to be hurt; you understand that he's going to come for you now."

"I understand that more than you can know. And he's not going to pull a gun on me. He might be a lot of things, but he won't shoot me." Hudson took a bite of her roast beef and moaned while glaring at Storm. "I don't get a lot of home cooked meals, and you're taking my buzz away. I'm not carrying a gun."

"What if he comes after you and Liam? What will you do then? Try and run him down with your rig? I would, if you want to know the truth." She said that her dad was a prick but he'd not harm anyone. "Yes, he will, and he has. Recently."

"Not me." Ordan wanted to laugh, but was sort of afraid to. The two of them were about as funny as he'd seen in a while. And seriously upset. "Why don't you just sit down and leave me alone? I know what I'm doing."

"Do you? Well, perhaps you can explain to me why he shot at you a few weeks ago." The fork in Hudson's hand dropped and she stared at Stormy. "You were coming out of the department store just after you dropped a load. As soon as you were near your truck, shots rained down on you like it was the Fourth of July. You were nicked once, but otherwise all right because you took cover under the truck."

"It wasn't him." Storm nodded and handed her a photo. "Where did you get this? The police told me that they had no leads, that it was random."

"I have access to a lot of shit. This is the satellite picture from about ten minutes before you were shot at. These two...." Hudson was handed two more photos and Ordan watched her pale. "These are as shots were being fired. He's aiming right at you."

The photos were handed around, and Ordan saw the face of the man who was entering the empty building with a large satchel on his back. A gun case. He knew as well as Stormy did that it was what he was carrying. The next pictures showed the man leaning over the top of the building and firing at the semi below him. Ordan didn't like this. This was just wrong.

Poor Hudson. He knew that she'd thought it was her dad but had not wanted to believe it. He found himself getting up to go to her, to comfort her, but Bri put her hand over his and held him tightly.

Let Liam do this, dear. She looks so lost right now. He told her it broke his heart. *Mine too. Stormy told me that she was going to have to get real with the girl. I wasn't sure what she meant, but she said that she needed to understand this wasn't a father to protect. Hudson needs to see him for what he is.*

I think she does now. He watched her as Liam held her. No tears for this one, but he could see her anger begin to boil up. Ordan would bet anything she was slow to burn, but epic when she let her temper go. He wondered when was the last time she'd erupted like he thought she might.

"I was having supplies come up missing from my truck. Nothing much. Just a case of water and some of those dried packages of food — well, calling it food is a gross overstatement — but I just thought I'd counted wrong." Hudson looked at Liam as she continued. "The police asked me if I had any reason to believe that someone wanted me dead. And my dad was the first person I thought of. He just popped in my head like I'd been thinking it for some time. But I thought there was no way he'd kill his child. I guess I was wrong."

No one said a word, but Ordan knew they were thinking what he was. She'd been lured there by the theft so that he'd have a shot at her. Ordan wondered what had happened that he'd go to such extremes. As soon as she started talking again, he had his answer.

"I pressed charges against him. It was the only way I could keep my license and work." Ordan thought that worse had been done for less. "He called me a few days after and demanded to know why I'd do that to my own dad. He didn't demand, but sort of whined at me. He's good at that, making everything look like it's not his fault. I asked him why he'd done what he had to me, and his answer was that he needed it. Just that, no other reason. And he didn't even have the decency to tell me he was sorry or that he'd pay me back. I lost it all because of him."

"He's going to get his ass in deeper than he can get out of soon. The Feds have been looking for him for a couple of weeks now. He hasn't paid any of his taxes for the last ten years. There is also the matter of firing his weapon in a public place, and the attempted murder of you. Also, the trouble that he's in with a couple of truckers that I know. The extra set of books is going to get him convicted on a couple of other things too." Hudson asked Storm why she'd told the other truckers about her problems. "I didn't do anything. Not at all this time. They know you as well. One of them is Benjie, and the other one is Betty Boop. I did want to ask you if that was her name or not."

"No, it's not. And you don't want to know how she got that handle either." They all laughed when Hudson shivered. "Aunt Eunice is on her way here. She'll know things about my dad that might help you track him down. I don't want a thing to do with him. I mean, even before this I had been avoiding him. I have a cell number too, but I don't think that's going to do you much good."

After giving Storm the number, they sat down to enjoy the

rest of their dinner. It was slightly somber now, but his lovely mate saved the day. She brought up the wedding, and then Nikki took over. He loved that his sons were all getting mates, but he wanted grandchildren, darn it. Of course, Andi and Mac were helping him out on that one, but it was one out of the six of them. They needed to get busy.

As they were walking their children to the door later that night, he still chuckled a little about Nikki convincing Hudson to be her bridesmaid. She'd argued that she didn't know her that well and Nikki said it didn't matter, they had a long time to get to know each other. It was getting her in the dress that he thought was going to be funny. Hudson said she wasn't wearing one. He had a feeling that they'd all be decked out that day and the best of friends by then.

"Poor little girl. To think her own daddy would do something like that." He sat on the couch with Bri and told her how he'd deal with the man. "Yes, me as well. But I think that beating him would only make it worse. He needs to fear her."

"Well now, she is a tiger now. She's not had the occasion to change yet. Liam said she was waiting until she was in a better frame of mind. He said that he was trying to take his time with courting her." Bri said she thought that was an excellent idea. "How is that going to get us a grandbaby, I ask you? Having one on the way is wonderful, and I'm looking forward to it like you'd not believe, but there are six of them boys, and all but one is married off now."

"Give them time." He just stared at her. A week ago she had been on a buying spree that set them back a few pennies, now she was saying to wait? He asked her what she was playing at. "I'm not playing at anything. I'm just thinking that once the new baby gets here, they'll all see how much we love it and give us more."

27

"I think you're playing me." She just laughed and he smiled. He surely did love this woman, and didn't think that he'd ever get enough of showing her how much. "I've been thinking. You and me, we need to go on a nice trip. How about one of those cruises where we can eat until we pop, and see the sights?"

"You would think of food first. I don't want to leave until this thing with Emma is over." He nodded, thinking that he might want to meet her daddy himself. "Also, her aunt is coming. I think she's going to be someone who brings Emma out of her shell too."

"She sounds like she could hunt bear with a switch and come out on top. I tell you, I think she might be scarier than my Stormy." Bri agreed. "But she does sound as if she loves that girl, and she can't be all that bad, right?"

"Not bad at all." She sat there for a few more minutes and he just looked at her. Ordan considered himself the luckiest man on earth when he'd found her as his mate. And when the boys came along, he wasn't sure how he was able to walk around with his heart so full. "Ordan, do you suppose we'll make good grandparents? I know we've talked about this before, but I do worry so. There are so many rules now that we didn't have when we raised the boys."

He wanted to tell her that she was nuts for thinking that they'd not be perfect, but he'd been reading up on being a grandda too. It wasn't as easy as he'd thought it would have been. There were more things out there that would hurt a baby. Like baby powder, of all things.

"I think you and me will give it the best we can, and hope if we mess up too much—not that I think we will—but I do hope that they'll let us know and we'll change it up. I'm not going to be going against them on the important things they teach their kids, but I'm planning to spoil them rotten. To a point." She smiled at him and he thought he was gonna bust with love. "I want to go on trips with them. Take them places we took the boys, and buy them what they need and want. No socks from us."

"No, no socks. I can still see Riordan's face when he got socks and underwear from your mother that year. I don't think he ever opened the packages either. He was heartbroken that she had asked him what he wanted, then gotten him something as mundane as socks. I don't even think they were the right size." Ordan said he'd told her several times what he wanted. "I know, but she had her own set of rules. I hate to say this, Ordan, but your mother wasn't a nice person."

"No, she wasn't. Not one bit. And I thought for sure once the grandbabies came along, she'd mellow out. But I think for sure that it made her meaner. Darnedest thing, my mother. She wouldn't have been happy even if you'd have given her everything she ever wanted." He thought of his mother more and more of late. Just thinking about what she'd think of all these boys having mates. "She'd find so much fault with them that I think I'd have to turn her out. Or have her taken out. That Stormy, she'd not take any guff from her…none of them would, I think. It would be a sight, I'm telling you, my love, to have been able to see her trying to bring them to her heel."

"I think that any one of those daughters of ours would take care that she straightened up her act. My goodness, even Andi would have put poison in her food if she treated her badly." He laughed with Bri. "But the fact that we don't have grandchildren yet, I can wait. I think once it starts to happen, we'll have more than we ever hoped for."

The doorbell going off made him stand. It was late, much too late to be having company coming around. When he heard the woman's voice in the front hall, he had a feeling that they were about to meet Eunice Clarke.

"I'm at the wrong house? How do you figure that, young man? I was brought here by the cabbie. I said take me to the Harrison house, and this is where he brought me. Do you know where you are?" He laughed when he heard sputtering, and almost felt sorry for Jim as he went into the hallway to greet the person. "I'm looking for the Harrisons. Really, I'm searching for my niece, Emma. Goes by that god-awful last name of hers, but then I guess it's all right. Who are you?"

"Ordan Harrison. This is my wife, Bri. Emma isn't here right now. I mean, they don't live here. But you're more than welcome to stay with us until she returns." Jim took off toward parts unknown, and Ordan had to laugh a little. "You sure do stir the pot, don't you? Emma, she told us you were a force to be reckoned with. I guess she got that part right."

"I just found out about what my good for nothing brother, Burt, did to her. Is she...? Well, she said that one of your boys, I'm assuming, changed her." He told her that it was Liam. "You better know right now that he'd better be good to her, or I'll have his cat fur laid out in front of my fireplace. She's had enough shit going on in her life, and she doesn't need some asswipe of a man taking her to task about things. Where are they?"

"They were headed out tonight for a backhaul, I think she called it. I don't think she expected you for a few more days. I'd be honored if you stayed with us. I know that Liam and her just bought them a home, but it's going to need some work done on it before they can move in." She said she'd be glad to have somewhere to stay. "Good. That's good. I'll have your things taken up. Are they here?"

"Yes. I had to take a cab here. They're out front on the porch.

And if you think just because I'm old that I can't do for myself, I'll show you a thing or two myself." He told her he'd never think that. "I'm glad to hear it. I'm supposing that I've missed supper. Well, I guess I can order me a pizza or a hoagie. Don't want to put anyone out any more than I have to."

"We can have the cook fix you up."

He darted away from her toward the kitchen when he saw Bri come out into the main hall a little more. He was nearly caught when she called him back to see what they might have. Christ, she was worse than they thought she'd be, in a stern sort of way, and Ordan thought he might grow to like her. Maybe.

Chapter 3

Liam had no idea what he'd expected when they left his brother's drive, but he was enjoying himself. There was a great deal to see from this height, and he wasn't even intimidated by the other traffic as he usually was. He hated highways and the speed some people felt it was all right to go. He looked over at Emma when she asked him if he was all right.

"I am, as a matter of fact. This is my first time in a truck. At least that I can remember. My parents took us to see the firetrucks when we were boys, but this isn't at all like that." She grinned as they merged into another lane. "How do you know where to go?"

"I usually have GPS on my phone to guide me, but I've been to this place a few times so I know where I'm going. I have backhauled for them for years. They pay well, and when I get there, someone is always ready to take the trailer from me." He nodded and watched her drive. "I've been doing this for so long that I just take it all in stride. Winter is harder, as you can well imagine. And stupid drivers. They think that just because they're on the road, they own it. I've had my share of fender benders with this thing."

"I've seen a few terrible ones over the years too. Ennis, he's the doctor, he said that when a car is hit with a semi, no matter whose fault it might be, there is going to be someone killed. He's just gone out on his own and is away from those sorts of emergencies. I think he enjoys that the most." He leaned back, careful of the gear shifter that was between them. "Tell me about yourself. You tell me one thing and I'll tell you something about myself. It'll be a good way to get to know each other."

"I'm just a person. I mean, I have some quirks and peeves that I think annoy people. Like, I'm very neat and tidy. I think that is because of where I spend a lot of my time. With things having a place that they need to go back into, I've learned to clean up after myself more than normal." He asked her about her quirks. "I don't care for cereal. I know that sounds like nothing, but it is a big deal to me. I like eating a hearty breakfast. I don't get it often, not like I had at your parents' house, but I do like to start my day with one."

"I eat late. I mean, it's not usually considered breakfast when I get around to eating my first meal of the day." Emma asked him if he was a late sleeper. "No. I'm usually up by five in the morning, but I get up and get going. It's nearly noon when I get something to eat. And one of my pet peeves is people who wear jammies to the store. I know that it's a fashion statement, but I don't think it's a good one. But that's just me."

"Oh, how about people who use their carts as a weapon? You know the ones. They bump you out of the way when you're trying to decide on which mustard to buy." Liam laughed when she did. "Also, the people who block the end of the aisle to be sociable. Oblivious to all those trying to get around them."

"I call them enders. They'll stand there and glare, too, when you excuse yourself to get around them." He told her about the time he'd gone with his mom. "She finally had had enough of these two women who were shopping. At the end of each turn, they'd turn and look down the next one and try to see what was down there and if they might need it. Mom just lost it, I think. She told them that if they were going to shop like it was their job, they should ask the manager for a map on where everything was. Then she told them, none too politely, to get out of her way until she was ahead of them because she had six boys at home that were hungry. I don't think I ever remember seeing them in there again."

They were laughing so hard when she pulled over that he'd not even realized it had been several hours since they left the house. Going into the rest stop to go to the bathroom, he waited for her to come out when he was finished. Liam noticed that the people going in and out of the place were truckers too. Most of them were men, but there were a great many women too. And a few of them were talking to Emma when she came out to join him.

"If I see her, I'll let you know." The man nodded and walked away. "His wife is a tandem driver with her sister. Yesterday she left him for another woman. I don't think it'll end well."

"I see." He didn't, but followed her to the cart that was selling coffee and donuts. He noticed that all she got was a cup of hot water, and he did the same. Emma had some tea bags in her truck, and he figured that was what she was going to do. "I brought some of that tea that you liked from Mom's house. If you want."

"I have the cheapy stuff in the truck, but it's hard to heat water in the microwave. And since I have a few hours to kill, I thought I'd catch up on some computer work." He nodded and wondered what was going on.

She'd been so happy before, but now she seemed sort of sad,

almost depressed. He didn't know her well, not yet, but he'd bet this wasn't usual for her. As she sat at her makeshift computer table in the back, he chose the front passenger side and pulled out his own computer. He would wait to see if she wanted to talk about whatever was bothering her.

"If you want to talk to me while I work, that's all right." He nodded and opened the email from Big Ben. "I just have to make sure that I have my hours turned in for each drop and load. They'll deposit my checks through one of those online places. The longer I wait to give them an accounting, the longer it takes for me to get paid. Some of them are net thirty, while others pay right away."

"Do you ever not get paid?" She told him that it happened once in a while, but not often. "I heard from the contractor. He said that he'll start in the morning and have the walls in the kitchen out by nightfall. He wants to know what sort of kitchen we want. Normal, or do we want high end?"

"What's the difference?" He told her what he'd found out when his brother had redone his house. "Oh. I guess that makes sense. High end is more technical and normal would be pretty much standard stuff. I don't know. I cook, but not all that much. The rest of your family has live in help. Will you?"

"Yes, we will, if you don't mind. I work a lot, and you do as well, so I don't want to have to mess with the house upkeep and miss spending time with you. Then there are children. By the way, do you want any?" Emma told him she did. "Good. My parents will be very happy to hear that."

"Your dad all but measured my hips to see if I could birth big babies. He said that you weighed a whopping nine pounds and eleven ounces, and you were the lightest." He laughed and told her that Riordan weighted almost twelve. "Sheesh, your poor mom. And in answer to your question, I think we should research what we want. I don't believe for a minute that even though it's high end, it'll be perfect, do you?"

"No, I don't. I'll look into it now." Liam pulled up the list of items that Big Ben had sent him that they'd need. Not only kitchen items, but also the furnace, air conditioner, as well as flooring in some of the rooms. "How do you feel about hardwood floors in the dining—?" She moaned and he looked at her. She was reading what appeared to be emails now.

"My aunt is at your parents' house. And she has some information on Dad. She wants to know who she should talk to." He told her Stormy or Nikki. "Aunt Eunice said that she likes your parents, but she thought that your dad thinks she's an old woman. Would he say that?"

"Doubtful. My mom would have kicked his ass if he had." Liam laughed. "Is she going to stay with them until we return?"

"It appears so. She has a lovely room, she says here, and she is in love with the cook. Aunt Eunice says that we shouldn't be surprised if she takes her home with her when she leaves." When she laughed, he waited for the rest of the email to be told to him. "Aunt Eunice said that she's got her eye on a house close to the one we're building, and for us not to say a word if she helps us out with some wedding money toward some of the house problems."

"We don't need her money. I told you, I've done well for myself." Emma looked at him and he could see her sadness. "What is it, baby? Did someone say something to you in the bathroom?"

"My dad is looking for me. He's trying to get a network going to hunt me down. Two of the drivers I was talking to said that Dad told them that they weren't to tell me, he wanted to surprise me with a visit." He turned the computer toward her when he opened the email from Storm. It was the ad about them getting married soon, with a picture. "That'll make him come for me, for sure. I'm guessing that it's easy to figure out your family has money too."

"I don't think it's a secret, so I'm guessing he could, if he wanted to." She nodded and leaned into her computer. "Emma, why don't you forget that for a little while and come up here and let me hold you? Or I can come back there to hold you."

"I want to have sex with you." He nearly snapped his hand in the computer on his lap when she spoke. "I have no idea why, but the thought of having you make love to me sounds like the best medicine ever. Whatcha think?"

"I'm not sure what to think." Emma nodded, but didn't move. "I want you. So does my cat, but that bed, it's not all that big, is it?"

"No. It's only a twin." He nodded and tried to think how making love on a single mattress was going to work for them. He was well over six feet tall, and she wasn't short. "I guess we could wait until I drop this load, get a hotel room, and go from there."

"Or—and you can say no—we could get lost in the woods behind this place, shift, and have some fun. You've never been your cat yet, and this will be a good place to do it. You won't have to be afraid." She looked out the window, then back at him. "How long before we can get to a hotel?"

"Too long." He grinned. "How do I do this? I'm assuming that I have to be naked. And somewhere I can be that way so that no one sees me."

"I will." He felt his cock stretch in his pants. She stood up and climbed over the seat and stood outside the truck. "We're going now?"

"Yes." She threw her jacket in the truck and started for the wooded area behind the rest stop. She was nearly halfway there when she turned to look at him. "Well? Are you going to stay here or come with me?"

"Christ." He nearly killed himself falling out of the big rig, and was chasing after her when he realized what they were going to do. Shift, yes, but he hoped they were going to bond as well. As soon as he caught up with her, he took her hand in his and pulled her to a stop. "This will make us one. I want you to know that going in. When we make love, and we will, I want you to know that this will make us a bonded couple. Forever."

For an answer, she pulled him to her mouth and kissed him. Liam pulled her body to his to let her know how much he wanted her, needed her. His cock ached to take her now, and when she jumped a little in his arms and wrapped her legs around his hips, Liam moved them toward the woods. He had to let her go after a few steps or fall with her to the ground. Then they'd never get up. Holding her hand, they nearly sprinted to the woods.

~~~

Hudson was giddy. There were no other words to use to describe how she was feeling right now. The being inside of her, the cat that she could become, had been touching off emotions and feelings within her for hours now, and she wanted to let her out. Then there was the big hunky man in front of her.

Liam was successful, rich, and kind. He was also sexy, tall, and had a voice that sent chills down her body that seemed to center in her pussy. He could be talking about the weather and she'd still find herself wet with it. Christ, she had it bad for this man. As soon as she got to see him naked, Hudson knew that she'd feel better about her life in general. And if he touched her with the same kind of sexiness of his voice, she knew that she was never going to be the same again.

"You have to know that I can read your thoughts." She giggled. "Christ woman, you're killing me, and I've done nothing but hold your hand. I swear, I could come right now and then take you several times."

"Promise?" He stopped so quickly that she hit him from behind. But instead of letting her go, he pulled her to his body and kissed her. It was hungry, demanding, and oh so delicious. "Are we there yet?"

"Yes." He pulled his shirt up and over his head. She had a moment to admire the furred chest, the hard nipples. Then he bent at the waist and pulled his jeans and boxers off. When he stood up, kicking his pants and shoes off his feet, Hudson had to hold onto the tree behind her or fall. "Strip. If you don't, then I'm going to do it for you and there won't be anything left salvageable once I do."

"I'll wear your shirt back." He nodded and took a step toward her, and she felt her pussy soak. "Hurry, Liam, I'm ready now."

The sound of tearing cloth made her moan. The breeze, cooler than her body, made her breasts ache and burn. Her shirt was off before he pulled her to him again, and she cried out when he tore her pants off. Standing naked before him, she turned and let him have his fill of her.

"I can't wait for my cat to take yours." She nodded. Moving toward the tree again, she leaned against it and spread her legs. "I can smell you. Both of us can. I'm sorry, love."

Before she could ask him for what, his cat was there. Large and tawny looking, the black stripes of him faded out in the night. The glow of his eyes, the size of his body didn't frighten her at all. But when he moved his big head between her legs and licked her, Hudson screamed then covered her mouth with her hand when she came four times, hard, in a row.

He never hurt her but did nip at her flesh, licked her over and over until her knees were weak with it. When he backed up, she slid to the ground and he pounced on her like a feast. She came several more times, his tongue fucking her hard enough that she was dizzy with it. Finally, after begging him several times to stop, to let her catch her breath, she felt the difference and knew that Liam was back.

I love the way you have given yourself to us. The voice in her head had her sitting up. "You and I can communicate that way. It's like our own private cell phone number with graphics if you want. You can with all my family now as well. Just think of them and you can talk."

"If it's all the same to you, I'd rather not talk to your parents or any of them right now." He laughed and she smiled. "Liam, please. I need to feel you inside of me. I beg of you to do something, or I'm going to have to hurt you."

He moved up her body, nipping at her skin, licking her heated flesh. She came twice more, once when he licked her belly button, the second time when he bit her nipple. By the time he was at her pussy, his mouth doing things to hers so that she wanted to smack him to take her, she was on edge, and felt her cat begging her to let her go.

Liam slid inside of her just as she was thinking of letting the cat take her. He held himself stiff above her, her body primed for.... She wasn't sure what it was holding onto, but she could feel it, almost touch it. And when he moved his tongue along her pounding pulse, Hudson held her breath, waiting for whatever he had given her to take her. And when it did, she screamed.

His teeth were sharp and the bite was painful, but not enough to make her wish he'd not done it. It was beautiful the way he tore into her flesh. Hudson thought she'd never forget this for as long as she lived.

Releasing the pressure, or so it seemed to her, only opened the door to more feelings, more need. And when he took her harder, pounding at her body like he was mad with his own need, Hudson wrapped her legs around him and pulled his throat to her mouth. Her mouth felt wider, her teeth were moving on their own.

"Bite me." She did, sinking her teeth into his throat until she tasted blood, felt it fill her throat and mouth with the elixir of the gods. "I love you."

She felt her world tilt then just slip away. Even as he cried out with his own release, she held onto him, knowing that when she blacked out, he'd protect her. Then she felt nothing.

Waking, she found his large tiger beside her, his body close enough that she didn't feel the chill. Rolling to her side, putting her arm over him, Hudson felt like she could take on the world and come out on top. His soft laughter made her pull his fur a little, and he stretched out beside her and laid his head on her belly.

We didn't get to run. She nodded, feeling much too good to let anything bother her. *If you want, we can run for about a half hour before we have to go out again.*

"How do I do it?" Liam told her to think of the cat and when she saw her, ask her to take her. "Ask her? She's been beating me up trying to take me for hours."

She might have thought it was time, but until you're ready or need her, she wouldn't have made you. Nodding, she stood up and Liam licked her breasts. *I can't let an opportunity like that go by.*

She saw her there when she closed her eyes. The cat was beautiful. Her colors were brilliant, and her eyes the same purple hue as hers. And when she bowed before her, just laid her head down on the ground in front of her, Hudson asked her to come forth.

The tightening of her skin told her that she was shifting. While it wasn't painful, as she thought it would be, it was strange. As soon as she opened her eyes again, she saw things differently.

I can see other animals, but not like I see them as me. More of a...I can see their heat, their body outlined in heat. He asked her if she could make out what they were. *Yes, I see a bird, and a deer grouping not far from here. There is also.... Oh my goodness. There is a man having sex with another person. Another male.*

I can't do that. She looked at him and blinked several times when she could only make him out as a heat signature as well. *Emma, can you see anything like its true self?*

No, not even.... Am I to assume that this isn't something you can do? He told her he didn't think any of his family could. *I don't understand then. How come, as a converted cat, I can?*

I'm not sure. But with each person, there is always some sort of special thing they can do. A protective skill, you might call it. She looked around again, afraid now of her cat. *She's very beautiful. And big. Almost as big as my cat is.*

She's not like you, though. I don't understand that. He said he didn't either, but it was all right. Her cat would help her to understand why. *I'm afraid, Liam. What if your family doesn't like that I can do this?*

Why would you think that? I mean, they already love you to pieces. As much as I do, I think. No, they'll just say that you're special, and until they have a need for your skill or you do, then they'll just take it in stride. He nudged her with his head. *Come on, let's have a run before we have to get back to work. I don't know about you, but I'm having a wonderful time doing this with you. I can't do it all the time, but I love it.*

She did as well. But if she was honest with herself, she was growing tired of being on the road all the time. And had been for some time. Not the money or the meeting of the people, but just driving all day long with no one to talk to or to have a nice dinner with.

When he took off running, Hudson did as well. It was odd for a few moments trying to make her feet run in the right order. After falling twice in a row, she took her time learning to walk on four feet rather than just two. After that, she couldn't get enough of leaping and running through the thick forest. It wasn't until she came to a cooling heat signature that she paused in her fun and called to Liam.

The body lying there was still, but cooling fast. Making her way to it, she was careful to look around before seeing Liam coming toward her as a man. He had his pants on and his shirt in his hand. And he was on the phone. This was going to make her late, she just knew it.

CHAPTER 4

Liam waited for the police to release him. They had let Hudson go because he was willing to stay behind, but he knew that she hadn't wanted to leave him. But it was all right with him. He didn't have any more information than she did on what had happened, and the fact that it was a female ruled out the two men that she'd seen earlier.

"There is no identification on the body. No clothing, nor a purse. You didn't touch anything, did you?" He told the officer that he had not, other than to see if she had a pulse. "What was it again you were doing out here?"

"Having sex." The man said nothing but nodded, and didn't make a crude comment as the other cop had done. "We're getting married soon and I'm riding with her on this trip. Or I was until this occurred."

"Liam, I don't think you had anything to do with this, or your girlfriend. But we have to be sure." Liam said he understood, and if it was his family, he'd want all the information he could find as well. "I've spoken to your sisters. Nikki and Stormy Harrison have called me three times since I was called here. They surely are protective of you, aren't they?"

"Family." He nodded again. "We came across the body and

called you guys. I don't think we were any more than a few feet from it when we were headed back to the truck."

"We have the security tapes. We know when you both pulled in and called us. Even if you had the body on you and put it here, we would have seen it. We didn't." Liam said, again, that he'd had nothing to do with this. "I know. But as I said, we have to cover everything."

The woman had passed away just before the first cruiser pulled in the lot. Liam had tried to help her, but she was too far gone before he could do much more than hold her hand while she breathed her last breath. The officer asked him if she'd said anything.

"No, I don't think she could have, do you?" The officer shook his head, and Liam looked to his left and saw Mason standing there. "I know you're not human. I have a friend here that can help you if you'll allow it."

"Vampire? You think he might have done this?" Liam didn't take offense, and neither did Mason when he stood beside them. "If you can help me, even to identify her, that would go a long way in finding out what the hell happened here."

Mason made his way to the young woman. Her body had been torn up, her throat ripped out. Her clothing was intact, but little else was. Both arms had been broken in several places. Her belly had been eviscerated; her internal organs looked as if they'd been dragged from her body, or she had moved and they had spilled out. Her left leg looked as if it had been yanked from her hip, and the other was as broken as her arms. Whoever had done this to her had been angry, he'd bet, and wanted her to suffer in ways that were just too profound to think about.

"It wasn't a vampire. Nor was it a shifter of any kind. A human man did this to her. And as strong as the scent is, I would

46

imagine that he's not far." They looked around at the crowd of people that had begun to gather when the police did. "If you would be so kind as to stand right here, I'll have a look."

He was gone before either him or the cop could say yes. There were perhaps thirty people there, and with the sun coming up, there would be more once they noticed the ambulance and cruisers in the lot. As soon as he returned, Mason said that the man was no longer there but had gotten into a vehicle on the other side of the lot, the trucker side. Liam asked him where.

"Your mate was not near him." Liam fell to the ground, his relief was so profound. "He isn't going to get far, I don't think. He has a very bad gasoline leak that if you would like, I can follow. But not any more than that. I'm afraid that the sun would surely make me too weak to help."

"Yes, please." Mason disappeared. Liam sat there for several seconds and thought of Hudson. He reached out to her but she told him not now. Driving through downtown traffic was hard enough without a man in her head. "My mate. She's a trucker, and I love her with all that I am."

"As it should be." Anthony Shane directed the coroner to the body after pictures were taken from every angle. "I would like to have you and the mate come in to my office when she returns. As I said, I don't think you had anything to do with this, but I still will have questions. Someone had a powerful amount of hate for this poor thing and we need to figure out who it is."

The coroner put both of the victim's hands in plastic bags. Then Anthony and the older man put their initials on the tape. One of the junior officers came back from the woods, his face a little pale, and told them he'd found where the girl had more than likely been hurt. Liam stayed where he was…there was no reason for him to go with them.

How are you doing, son? He told his dad what he knew. *I've been talking to Stormy, wanted you to know that she has you someone there to help you out. She said that while they're telling you that you're not a suspect, everyone is until proven otherwise. Also, I called in a few favors of my own and that girl of yours, she's got herself someone watching her as well.*

Thanks, Dad. I just spoke to her and she's downtown, which I think is close to where she had to go. He said he'd been cut off a bit ago and left her alone. *She's nervous, I think. And she didn't want to leave me.*

No, I don't think she would have liked that overly much. You just sit tight and let them do their jobs. They'll know what to do. He said that he'd do just that. *Good. And so you know, Hudson's aunt, she's been talking to that Ben person a bit. The house is now moving on a little faster than you thought. That woman, Eunice, she's a pistol, I'll say that about her. When she wants something done, it's gonna be or heads will roll.*

She told Emma that she was going to do something, but she didn't say what. To be honest, Dad, she sort of frightens me a bit. The aunt, not Emma. The stories Emma told me about her makes me think of Grandma when she was alive. His dad laughed. Mason appeared before him holding a man covered in blood. *I have to go, Dad. I think we might have the murderer.*

Standing up, he could smell death and anger on the man. He'd never equated the last emotion with a scent, not really, but now he could almost taste it. Sending the cop that had been with him to get Anthony, he wondered what would drive a person to do the things that had been done to someone else.

"He was just starting to clean himself up at the next rest stop." Liam asked him if he'd had any trouble with him. "A bit, but that's all right. I was hungry anyway."

Liam didn't comment. Mason was an old and very powerful vampire, and if he wanted to taste the man in front of him or the entire police force that was there, he'd do it and there'd be no one to stop him. Anthony came toward them, and he looked a little sick himself. Before he could pull his gun and no doubt use it on the man, Liam stepped between them.

"You can't." Anthony just stared at him. "You can't kill this man no matter how badly you want to. If you do, then no one will have justice."

"You don't know the carnage that we just found." Liam said he didn't, but that didn't make it right in killing him. "He did things to her, used things to hurt her that.... I can't imagine how that poor woman even survived for as long as she did."

Mason put the man to his knees and held him there. There was anger in his face as well, more than he'd ever seen on the vampire before. Even his eyes, usually a light shade of blue, were dark with red blood. A quick shake of his captive and the man started talking.

"I killed her." Anthony told him to wait. "All right. I want to confess it all. Just hurry. I can't hold it in anymore."

The video recorder was brought in and two of the several officers also had their phones out, recording what was going to be said. As soon as he was read his rights, the man started talking, starting out with the name of the woman and his own name.

"Her name is Margo. All I got from her. She didn't even have a fucking credit card on her. But my name is Richard Walton...I goes by Dick." Anthony asked him what had happened. "I was coming out of the pisser there and I seen her. She was a pretty little thing, and I asked her to come on out to my truck and we could have a little fun. They always say no to me. I don't know why, I'm a good-looking man. But she told me several times that

49

she was waiting on someone. When this here feller comed out of the pisser, she started off with him, but I wanted me some fun so I killed him first. He's out there yonder too, if you want to look. There ain't much to him left. I don't know why she was fighting me either. I'm a good fighter too. But when she starts with her screaming, I told her to shut up and use her mouth for something more entertaining, but she said no. Like that wasn't part of the deal for me killing that fucker off."

"She tell you to kill the man she was with?" Dick said no, but it was necessary, he supposed. "So, you killed this other man and took her away."

"Well, I couldn't rightly take her to my truck, now could I? Christ, man. Think. She was screaming her fool head off by then and drawing attention. So, I popped her one in the head and drugged her off." Liam wondered if this man had done this before, and his next statement confirmed that he had, several times. "Usually I just have some fun with them, then throw them out of the truck down the highway. Nobody'll notice a spit of blood here or there, and the dogs or whatever take the rest away."

"This man, can you describe him?" He did, all the way to what he looked like when he'd finished with him. "You're saying that you killed him, just to have sex with the woman."

"Well, it wasn't just sex. I like to roll in them a bit before I take leave of them. They're not enjoying it no more, if you wanna know the truth of it, but I surely do." Liam rubbed his hand over his belly, feeling as sick as he'd ever been before as the man continued. "Anyhows, I been doing this for a long time now, and when this here man showed up and seen me washing up, I figured it was about time I got out of the business. I'm nuts, you see. Crazier than a two-legged horse in a race, I am. And that's what I'm gonna tell anyone that'll listen to me. I got me stories that will curl your milk and make your balls tight to your body, I do. And I'm not going to serve a single minute of prison on account'a I'm nuts."

~~~

Mason knew that the man was playing them. He'd seen it before. A man on a mission, so to speak, out to kill for the joy of it. And this man had killed a great many people in his lifetime on the road. He knew that should he speak to Liam on this that his young mate would know some of the names that this man had in his head. But this was too much, even for him, and Mason wanted to take matters into his own hands on this one. The only other person that he trusted was who he reached for now.

Please tell me you caught the mother fucker. The thought of him being out there is going to make me really pissy. And you, of all people, know how I am when I'm pissy. He laughed, the first one he'd had in several days. But then it was like that with Browning. *What's going on?*

I have him. But he is playing the fool. And quite nicely too. And you know some of my powers well enough that I can see what he will do should he live. She asked him if it was bad. *Yes.*

Kill him. He said that as much as he'd like to accommodate her, he could not. *There's something else, isn't there? Something that you.... You're there with Liam and you can't tell him because of Hudson.*

He would have killed her instead of the woman that died. And they saw him, this man, murder the young man as well. Liam and his mate saw them and thought them to be having sex. They do not know it as yet, but they will when they see where the spot was that the murder occurred. She cursed better than any person he knew. And loudly. *I should like to know that justice has been served. Because should he go to trial, he'll continue what he has a taste for.*

And killing him isn't an option, or not one at the moment. He told

51

her where he was and what he was doing. *I see. So, I'm thinking that you should use some of the mojo you have and make the fucker kill himself. Or do something equally stupid and have one of the cops kill him. Being on tape is going to clear up a great deal of messiness where the good guys are concerned.*

I can do that. She asked him what else was going on. *The young tiger. She has an ability that I've never seen on a cat before. She can see heat from the living.*

I don't understand. You mean to tell me that she is like the infrared lights that the army uses? He said that was it. *Holy fuck a duck, Mason. They'll take her for that should that information fall into the wrong hands. Can you...? Christ. I'll talk to them when they get back. This is serious shit.*

I am aware of that. And you do not just have to worry about the army wanting her, but humans as well. They'll use her, then when she has given them what they need, they'll destroy her. Browning told him she'd figure this out, but to get rid of the man. *I will. Now, you shouldn't warn Liam. I think his reaction will play better should he be as surprised as the next.*

Mason knew that what he was doing would be considered murder to most. He really didn't care. He was someone that had been skirting the law, sometimes simply ignoring it, for his own personal gain. But not with this. This would harm his family, and that was what he considered the Harrisons to be. Family.

This had to be timed, and perfectly. He wanted none of this to fall back to harm young Liam. He enjoyed his company and thought him to be a good man, with a kind heart. He also liked Hudson. She not only could hold a conversation on many subjects, but she had a way about her that put a person at ease faster than he could with his magic. He reached into the mind of Walton and frowned. This might be harder than he thought.

You'll get away from me. Toss me to the ground and take off running. He'd tasted the murderer, and while he found his blood to be tainted with evilness, he'd been hungry and needed him. But it wasn't easy getting through to him…his mind was a jumble of plans to murder Hudson. *You will listen to me. Knock me back and run. It will be your only chance to get to her.*

"I'm going to kill her. Kill her. Then I'm going to roll in her blood as I come."

Mason found himself on his back, his body hurting from the impact. But before he could stand up, the killer was dead. Several bullets tore through his body even as he fell to the ground.

It had taken the police less time than he thought it would to react. They were primed for him to be dead, so that was more than likely the reason. The man that had murdered more people than would ever be found was finally stopped, and Mason didn't feel the least bit sorry for his part in it.

I'm sorry. He asked Browning why. *I think you asked me if you should murder him, and I didn't give you the answer you wanted.*

No, I wanted him dead. What I wanted from you wasn't permission, but someone I could trust to know that I had no choice. Even in his death, his thoughts were for Hudson. And her death would have harmed us all. Especially Liam. I think him to be more in love with his mate than all of the rest of you together. You all love, that is true, but this goes beyond anything I've ever come across before. Love times infinity, I think. He also seems to have a better handle on it. As in, he allowed her to leave him here to deal with this so that she'd not lose her job. How many of the other cats would have done such a thing?

None. He smiled as he made his way back to the building that Ennis used as his new offices. *Mason, why do you hang around here? I know for a fact that you have this big fucking mansion. You also have more money than even the Harrisons do. Why here? Why with us?*

I was thinking on that just today. I believe it is because I find you to be tasty. She laughed, which was what he'd hoped for. *I hung around here because of you, at first. Then the more that I was with the rest of your family, I realized what I might have been missing all these years by being alone. I have no other friends that I trust as much as you. There is no one that I would come out into the sunlight for but this family. I think of them as my own family.*

Yes, I'm sure that you love hanging out with a bunch of pissy women and bad kitties. He laughed as he lay down. *Good night, my friend. And thank you for today. I'll have to think of something to repay you with.*

All that I need is here. Being with you, Browning. She told him that she loved him. *And I you, my child. Forever and a day.*

Just before closing his eyes, he reached out to the rest of the Harrison ambush. They were all well and safe. He knew that someday he was going to have to tell them what he'd done, taken a little of each of them, even those that had not offered, to keep them safe. And so that he could find them. Mason wasn't going to let anything happen to them if he could help it.

One of the houses that he owned, the very one that Browning had been talking about, was the place of his birth. He hated the place with all that he was. There were no good memories of the household. Nothing there that he would cherish. And the dead, the ones that had lived and died there, were nothing to him long before they took their last breath. Reaching for Liam, he smiled when he realized that he was waiting for his mate.

I have a home I should like for you to sell for me. He said he could do that. *Of course you can. It is a mammoth of a place. A castle, I would think some would call it. It no longer is of use to me.*

Where is it? I can go there sometime after the wedding and check it out. Take some pictures. Do you know how much you were going to ask? He said that he did not. *All right. I'll look into the real estate in the area. How many acres does it have?*

Ah yes. Well, I should like to sell the town that I own that is a part of the estate. Will that be a problem for you? Liam said that it wouldn't. *Good. The estate, without the town proper, is about ten thousand acres. The castle is large, as I said, and has been modernized over the last few years. I believe there are a dozen bedrooms with baths. A large kitchen. I think at one time it was my plan to turn it into a lovely bed and breakfast. My parents would have hated it.*

I see. He more than likely did, Mason thought. *I can see what I can do. Perhaps I can go there and use it for a few days as a honeymoon stop. I'd like to travel a little with Emma, and she might enjoy that.*

After making arrangements for them to get together, Mason willed his body to rest. There was a great deal going on in his mind right now, too much for him to relax properly. So, after lying there for an hour, he got up.

His need for sleep wasn't as great as it had been many decades ago. In fact, countless things weren't as needed as they had been. Someone to watch over him had been his biggest investment of late. Cameras and computers had given him the ease of resting someplace without the bother of worrying. Going to his computer now, he looked around his domain and laughed.

The castle in Winter, England was much more ornate than any other house that he owned, and he thought that selling it would be a way to get it out of his life. His parents, younger than him when they met the sun, had collected. There was no rhyme or reason to their collections. There were a few hundred tea cups, most with saucers, some without. As far as Mason remembered, they'd never been used by his mother. His father had collected pipes for a little while, and never smoked, as far as Mason knew.

There were countless chairs in the place. Some of them

were even hung on the walls when it was apparent there wasn't anywhere else to store them. Mason remembered one room that had paintings in the seats of the chairs that hung on the walls as hangers. It was odd indeed.

And all these "treasures" of theirs, no one was to touch them or use them. In his youth, living with them, he had been forbidden to even use one of the chairs at a function, because it was one that was favored. Mason knew that he'd never been a favorite to either of them.

The computer showed him the grounds around both this house and the castle. There wasn't much in the way of gardening at the latter of the two. He never thought it necessary to spruce up a place that he despised. As he moved through the rooms via his camera, he thought of what Liam had told him about a honeymoon getaway. He decided then and there he was going to give the castle to the couple as a wedding gift when they returned. Provided that they liked the place.

"If not, then I shall burn it to the ground." He wouldn't, but it was a nice thought. "I need to get rid of baggage. I've held onto it long enough."

He rarely talked to himself. But when he wanted to work things out, he thought saying it aloud was better than just thoughts. The sound of his voice made it sound more final, he supposed, and with this, he needed things to be finished. Mason made his way to his sitting room and closed his eyes for a moment.

Mason was tired. Not just today, but in all things. He wanted to go, leave behind his life and be no more. He'd tried several times over his lifetime to end his way of living. But none of them had done what he wanted. But when Browning had kept him from his final resting place, she'd made him promise that he'd not try such a thing again. Ever. And that promise was enough to hold him here…for how long he had no idea, but he wasn't to die, by his hand anyway, until she freed him. Which for some reason he thought was going to be much longer than he'd ever thought. Browning was very stubborn.

CHAPTER 5

The wedding of a lifetime. That's what the papers had called it. Hudson didn't know if that was an apt name for it. She could think of a lot of other things to call it. Pain in the ass of a lifetime? Dress up in uncomfortable clothing wedding nightmare? Or even toe pinching shoes worn to the wedding of a lifetime?

"Stop fussing." She glared at Bri, then changed it to a smile. "Nice save, but I saw that. You don't care for dressing up, do you?"

"This is not dressing up. This it dressing to kill. Why is it so tight? I can hardly breathe." Nikki laughed and said that she had nowhere to hide her gun. "Gun? Can I borrow it? I'd like to shoot the person that designed this sucker."

"It's a lovely design. You girls should dress up more and you'd feel better about it when the time came. Look at Andi, she's not complaining." They all looked at the woman who sat in the chair eating a piece of pie that she'd brought in. "She looks lovely because she knows it."

"She is wearing a dress that is, while like this one, not skin tight. And her shoes are flat. Why do we have to wear heels?" Bri told her she was whining. "Of course I am. I have on shoes with heels that are two feet long and are shoving my toes out the tip of a hole the size of a quarter."

"It's not that bad. And they're not two feet, but only six inches. They make your legs look wonderful." Hudson huffed. "What do you think Liam is going to say when he sees you dressed up like this?"

"He'll wonder what sort of drugs I'm on. And if he thinks, even for a moment, that I'm going to dress like this again, he's nuts." Bri just laughed and kissed her on the cheek. "You know, that might work on your husband, but it doesn't on me. I hate this."

The wedding was going to be beautiful. And even though she fussed a great deal, Hudson liked the dress. It was a little tight, and every single breath made her think that if she had to sneeze very hard, she was going to bust out of it. It was long, falling to the floor long, and in the prettiest shade of lavender she'd ever seen. All of the bridesmaids were dressed in pastel colors that suited them to perfection. Storm was in a pale red. Not pink, but a nice shade of red. Andi in a sort of lemony green color. Brooke, who she'd only just met today, was in a grey that was a perfect foil for her light skin tone. But it was the bride that took the cake.

Nikki looked like a cake topper. It was silly, she supposed, to think that's what she looked like, but the dress was beautiful. The dress had been Storm's Aunt Sally's. And Hudson had to wonder how much it had cost her all those years ago.

The dress was an ivory color, with an open bodice that was covered in small pearls made to look like small flowers all over it. The straps were also designed with pearls that made her slender frame look even more beautiful. It was a full dress, like they used to wear long ago, with a long heavy train. The dress was made for being showy, and there wasn't a more beautiful bride than Nikki.

"You all right?" Nodding, she looked at Brooke. "You look like you're about to explode. I know how you feel, by the way. I hate dressing up as well. The only time I do is when I have a show. And even then, I've kicked my shoes off someplace and have to spend a good hour hunting them down. But I don't do it often."

"I feel so out of place. Not just dressed like this, but in this family. I'm not like you guys." She asked her why. "Well, you're this famous potter and artist. Storm is well known for her kick ass sort of storming through people. Not to mention, she's a decorated war hero. Nikki is related to the president, her husband to be is going to be president someday. Andi cooks like it's the easiest thing in the world, and makes everyone beg for seconds."

"And you? You're a driver that can drive something that none of us can." Hudson snorted. "You can. I've seen drivers come up my mountain with nothing more than a crudely drawn map, and back into my shed like it's out in the open and not centered around several trees, a house, as well as two outdoor kilns. You can, I'm betting, do better."

"That's just it, you see." Brooke said that she didn't. "You're all famous, wonderfully talented women. I'm a trucker. I move merchandise that I could never afford on my income to the stores that you guys go in and buy whatever you want."

Brooke sat down next to her and took her hand in hers. "What do you see here? I mean, besides the tiniest wrist I've ever seen."

"A ring." It wasn't just a ring either, it was an engagement ring that Liam had given her that morning before they left his parents' house. "It's a lovely, expensive engagement ring that the man that I love gave me."

"Yes, he did. Liam is in love with you too. All of us are. And even though I've only just met you, I love you as well. We're family. No matter what we are, what we can do, or even what our income was before meeting these Harrison men, we're first and foremost family." At a loss for words, Hudson leaned her head on the other woman's shoulder. "You have to come to our mountain. I can get you feeling pretty good about yourself in no time. I bet by the end of your visit, you won't wanna leave."

"I'm going to stop driving after this last load." Brooke asked her if that was what she wanted. "Yes, I want to be home when Liam is. Driving paid the bills, but I don't...I don't like to say that I don't need to work anymore, but I don't need to drive anymore. It's hard work, and there are a lot of nuts out there. I guess you heard about the guy at the stop we were at."

"Yes, I heard. I'm glad to hear that he's been dealt with, too." Hudson had her own theory on what really happened with him being killed, but kept it to herself. "You okay now? I mean, you seem less wiggy, as my grandda used to say."

"Yes, I'm all right now. I guess I'm overwhelmed. I mean, I've been to weddings before, but none where the President of the United States was giving away the bride." They both laughed and looked at the door when it opened. "I guess we're ready to get this party going, right?"

"Good luck, Hudson. Are you going to go by that or are you going to go by Emma? Not that I don't like both names, but it is sort of confusing for some of us to call you one name and the rest of us the other." Hudson said she was working on it. "Good. Just let me know. I'm so glad to have you as a sister, Emma Harrison."

The wedding was all that it was said it was going to be, beautiful and classical. The newspapers all over the world had been talking about it for the last few days. Mostly how the bride and groom were so lovely, that they had a nice home, and wealth that made their life a fairy book tale. The president being there had been a big deal up until yesterday, when he was ousted by a sneak peek at the dress that Nikki was going to wear. The press even speculated on how beautiful their children would be. Then the article had ended with Aedan's aspirations of following his new uncle to the White House. Hudson wondered what they'd say today if they were here. More than likely more of the same.

No doubt they'd be talking about the lavish gifts that were there as well. The senators that had come as well as heads of states. There were foreign dignitaries as well as a king and queen. Everyone that was anyone was in attendance. And Hudson was right in the middle of it all.

Making her way up the aisle, she looked at Liam. To her, he was by far the best looking of all the brothers. Smiling, she thought of the way he'd helped her into her dress to come here, then how he'd helped her out of it again just before the limo had arrived. His cat had brought her five times before Liam took his turn. Hudson had been as limp as an overcooked noodle, as her Aunt Eunice was fond of saying. But she'd not thought once of the wedding and her role in it the entire time. He was good at distracting her from things she didn't want to deal with.

The ceremony itself took less time than it did for them to walk up to the clergy. It ended with an announcement of the couple now being husband and wife, and a very long kiss. As Aedan and Nikki made their way down to the front of the church, Liam offered her his arm and she leaned on him. When he kissed her cameras popped everywhere, but she didn't care.

"Do you want a large wedding like this?' She told him no way. "Yeah, I figured you'd say that. If you don't mind, I've set us up in the chambers to get married before pictures are taken. Your aunt and my parents are going to be witnesses."

"Really?" He nodded. "That's wonderful. Thank you so

much. I love you, Liam." He kissed her again, and they were out of the church when she kicked her shoes off. "If I never have to wear heels again, I'll be a happy person."

An hour later, she was saying her own I do's, and was officially pronounced as Mrs. Emma Hudson Harrison. Liam was her husband. And she could not have been happier about it.

~~~

"Hey Burt. Congratulations." He nodded. That was the fourth time today that someone had said that to him. He didn't have the foggiest idea what the heck was going on, but wasn't telling these yahoos.

He sat down at the diner and ordered the special. It didn't matter what it was, and the only reason it was special was because he was sure there wasn't any one kind of meat in the dish. Everything in this place tasted like cardboard with brown goop on it. He missed having a nice dinner in a fine restaurant. Even some of the take-outs that he'd had when he'd been working was a damn sight better than this slop. As he drank his burnt coffee, he was told congrats again.

"You happy?" He told the waitress he was, as a matter of fact. "Sure is nice when your kids do better than you, don't you think? I wish mine had married money. All I got for them being married is another mouth to feed and more heartache than I ever had raising her up."

"Married? What are you talking about? I don't have any married kids. Why would you think that?" She handed him yesterday's paper. Right there on the front page was a wedding party. When he told her he didn't know anyone there, she pointed to the names at the bottom. Emma Hudson Harrison was third from the right. "Holy H. Christ. What the heck has she gone and done?"

He read the accompanying article. The big wedding had been the brother of the man she had hitched herself to. And from the looks of it, it must have cost more than he made in ten years. And darned if the president wasn't standing right there with them. The newspaper claimed he was the bride's uncle. As he read the rest of it, telling how the family was having a large celebration in the country club nearby, and that this Aedan person and Nikki were going to be honeymooning in the South of France for a month, he read about his daughter and her nuptials as well.

Spur of the moment, they called it. And much more to their liking. No big wedding for his little girl, he supposed. But the more he read of the article and the things that these people had their hands in, he was grinning. Why by golly, his daughter had done all right for herself. And him, he thought.

Money. She was going to be so rich that she was quitting her job, the paper said. Well, it didn't say that, but it did mention that she was not going to be a driver any more. Emma and her new husband were going to go on a short trip for a honeymoon and would be back in a few days. He looked at the article to read where this had all had taken place, and wasn't surprised to see it was in some podunk town in Ohio. The rich, he supposed, could live just about anywhere they wanted.

He was going to have to figure out a way to get back to her. She'd help her old man out. After all, he'd given her everything he had when he'd raised her up when her mom had left them. Burt shifted on the seat a little. He was pretty sure that Nora was watching him from a distance, keeping an eye on him in the event that he fucked up again. He had surely been surprised when she didn't come out of the woodwork when he took off, leaving Hudson with the bills he'd made.

"She's not going to be able to hold no grudge now that she's out from under all that." He sipped his coffee and grimaced. "She'll have some good food in her new digs, and money to burn. Enough to buy her old man some decent coffee. I'd like to try one of them bean kind. Not this dirt."

The special was set in front of him and he stared at it. Not that he wasn't going to eat it, but it didn't look like food. Gravy with something lumpy under it was all he could think of. And even the gravy didn't look all that appetizing. There was grease on the sides of the plate where it had cooled. Picking up his fork, he took a bite. Grabbing the catsup bottle, he drowned the food in it. He figured that if catsup couldn't fix food, then it wasn't worth eating. He didn't really think this it was going to help this time.

He needed a ride to Ohio, and figured if he buttered up Betty, she'd let him borrow her car to get there. He might even take her along, if she wanted to go. She wasn't as generous as some people he knew, but she liked him and would let him use her car again.

After an hour of trying to convince the waitress he would bring it back to her, he left. Some people just didn't know how to let things go. He'd only nicked the paint a little bit, and the fender was replaced by her insurance company when he'd backed into a wall in her car before that. Walking to the gas pumps, he asked around for a ride going to Ohio. When he finally found someone, he knew it was going to be a terrible ride. Just terrible. But then beggars couldn't be too choosy. Doug Sherman wasn't the best of people, not like him. The man was as sour as the lemonade he'd drank in the restaurant a few days back.

"I surely do appreciate you giving me a lift, Doug." The man nodded. He wasn't much of a talker, which didn't bother Burt much. He loved to talk. "My daughter just got herself married. Can you believe that? Her invite to me must have been misplaced."

"Is that what you're thinking? I don't. I don't think she likes you." He asked him why he'd say a fool thing like that. "You hurt her bad when you run off and left her holding your mess. I don't know why nobody has turned you in for hiding out here."

"Truckers' code." He thought of something. "You're not turning me in, are you, Doug? I mean, you don't have any kind of plans on doing that, do you?"

"Nope. Don't care enough about you to care if the cops find you or not. Does me a little bit good to see you going home." He thanked him. "I didn't say it was gonna be good on you, Burt. She's going to tear you up, I'm betting. That daughter of yours, she's a good girl, and I think she should be the one who turns you in."

Well that was just rude. Burt decided that he wasn't going to speak to Doug the rest of the trip. Course, he knew that wasn't going to work either, but he wasn't going to be a friendly with him. To say such a thing. He and his daughter had a good, solid relationship. And she'd do anything for him.

After ten minutes on the road, he'd had enough of the silence and turned to look at the other man. "My sister is there too. In Ohio. I don't know why she got her invite when I don't know where mine was. I guess I'll have to ask her about it." Eunice wasn't nice either, he remembered. She'd not done one nice thing for him in years. "Maybe we can work on patching things up with us too." Burt didn't expect an answer from Doug and didn't get one. Which suited him just fine.

Eunice had been mean to him since they were kids. He was older by a few years, and thought she should have been a lot nicer to her older brother. But she had a mouth on her that would sear a pork chop without ever touching a flame. And her eyeballing you when she was upset with something you did could make you want to squirm your way right out of her life. There had been that thing with her husband, somebody Clarke. He'd been bothering him since they got hitched, and Burt had shot him dead. The courts had said it was an accident, but Eunice hadn't seen it that way. She said he'd done it on purpose. He had, but she had no call in telling everyone that.

But she loved him too, despite being a bossy woman. Settling back in his seat, he tried to think why he'd not gotten an invite. It was strange that him, of all people, his only child's daddy, hadn't been there when she said her I do's. He sure hoped the man was nice and gullible. Burt needed some cash, and a lot of it, to be his father-in-law.

Could be she found out about the deals he'd been making. But them companies, they had insurance for those kinda things. He would bet any kinda money that they made more back on those runs he took than he got out of them. And boy oh boy, had he been living high when he sold them off. Frowning, he tried to think what the heck he'd done with all that money. Had fun, he knew, but he was sure it should have gone further.

He'd only backed up in one of them poor neighborhoods and opened his doors. He'd been surprised by some of the crap that he'd collected. The time he had a truckload of laundry detergent, he'd made a killing off it. And then there were the towels and washrags that he'd had. Toys too. A lot of toys went under some Christmas trees that year, he was betting. So in a way, Burt knew he was stimulating the economy.

Nobody knew where he was. He liked it that way for the most part. He'd been hiding out from the police on some silly little thing or another most of his adult life. And he'd gotten quite good at it, he thought. There was one time when he'd accidently broken into a gas station that had set him back some money.

Well, Hudson had bailed him out of that one. He smiled. She'd given him what-for on that one too.

"You know, kids are the best thing in the world. I mean, I have me the finest daughter that there ever was. When I mess up, which ain't as often as people think, she takes me back with open arms." Doug said something under his breath, but Burt didn't care. He knew the facts. "How long is it gonna be before we get to Ohio?"

"A week. I told you, I have a drop to make and then a layover for a backhaul." He nodded. "You gonna help me drive? You know, it would go a good deal faster in getting you out of my hair if you did."

"They went and took my CDL away. I'm gonna have to get that taken care of too. Or maybe not. Hudson, she married into some money, and she'll take care of her old man." Doug mumbled again, but Burt was happy. And if Doug couldn't be happy for him, then it was just plain his fault. "I'm thinking I could like me the life of leisure."

"You been living a life of leisure since I've known you." Burt grinned at the older man. "It weren't no compliment, Burt. You're about as lazy as they come. Why do you think she's gonna do a durn thing for you, Burt? You ain't been no good daddy to her. Never."

"She loves me just the way I am. And as her daddy, I know she'd want me to have whatever I need to make me feel better. Besides, I'm a working man, not lazy. I'm always working a deal where I don't have to work. There is a difference, Doug. I've strived my whole life in finding the easiest route. Looks like my daughter went and took after me on that. Married a rich man, and now she don't gotta trudge the roads no more." He was looking forward to living with her again. He might even help out around the house by keeping their staff busy all the time. "Yes, siree. I'm gonna love having her around me again. Missed her something terrible."

Burt thought about all the things he was going to do now that he had money. He needed to get him a car, not a used one either or a beater. He wanted brand new, something that he ordered. Then he was going to need some duds to wear. His jeans were as old as his car he'd lost in a poker game a few days back, he thought. Then he thought of her quitting the road.

It was too profitable to just up and quit. He knew that his little girl had money now, but he didn't want to have to go to her for every little thing. Burt wanted his own pocket money. Money he'd not have to beg for. Something he could flash around when he was out with his buddies. That was the ticket. He'd not spend it foolishly either, that's what Hudson's money was for. Burt was going to enjoy living the high life with his daughter. And there were ways of getting around all those restrictions they put on him too.

He'd use her rig again. Just for old times' sake. Burt decided that he'd go and get him a few loads, sell them off, and have some extra cash. Money in his pocket, and no one would be the wiser. 'Course, if they did, he'd just go into hiding again. Just until things blew over. Thinking again what he'd do with some money, he smiled.

A vacation. He'd bet anything that this man had himself a house somewhere on a beach where it was sunny all the time. Burt could see himself lying on one of them pink sanded suckers. Soaking up the sun and having them pretty little drinks with fruit and stuff hanging on the side of the glass. Of course, it wasn't like having a beer, but he thought he could surely change it up once in a while.

Asking Doug for a piece of paper and a pencil, he started making a list of things he was gonna need. And things he thought he could get out of his daughter. She'd do anything for him, he knew that. They were tight. He put on there that he'd need some spending money, just so he could get her something pretty when he was out. The list was getting longer by the mile, but he wasn't worried. He'd just have to make sure that the husband, now that she had one, understood that Burt was first in her life, or else. He wasn't above making sure she had insurance money too, for him and her.

Burt knew that he'd have to pare it down a bit once he got it all written down. There wasn't any sense in having himself a nice new car, not for everyday driving, when he was sure that the man would have a limo just for him. Then there was the pocket money. He decided that cash was just too cumbersome, and he'd have him give him a credit card. Not one with a limitless supply of money, he didn't want his new boy to go broke, but enough that he'd not have to borrow all the time.

The drop of the trailer was late. Much later than he'd thought it would have been. And when old Doug moved to the back end to rest up, he wondered where he was supposed to sleep. He thought when you were a guest of somebody, you gave up your bed for them. Apparently, old Doug didn't know that rule, and Burt decided to let it slide tonight. Doug had driven a while today. But tomorrow he'd point it out to him and take the bed. He might even go back there during the driving and take a few naps. It wasn't like Doug was using it.

Sleep was hard coming to him. It wasn't that he was uncomfortable in the seat, but there were also the plans he had just running through his head like a freight train. All the things that Hudson marrying had given him. Burt was gonna make her suffer some for not inviting him to the wedding when Eunice had been, but he wasn't going to hold out for too long. There wasn't no point in going too far. She had a temper on her, and sometimes she could be a bit harsh to her old man.

He surely wished that he'd not gotten that truck when he had. That had really put her in a bind, and she'd not been able to help him out. But he had asked her, several times, and she'd turned him down over and over. He'd bet anything that she was regretting that about now. Hudson loved him more than most daughters did their dads, and he loved it that way. She'd been powerfully mad when she'd found out that he'd used her house as the down payment. But by now she'd figured it out, and knew that her daddy was a smart man. He remembered her confronting him about the truck and the payments on it.

"Well, what did you expect me to do, darling? You only had one truck for us to use. And I had my heart set on something newer. I told you that." She asked him how he was going to make the payments on the truck. "You'll help me when I get a little behind. I got it all worked out. With the two of us working, half my income can go toward the truck and your half you put in will go toward the other half. Plus, since you've been working longer, you can chip in for gas and stuff. Don't even know why you need a house when we can live in style in one of these."

"You want me to pay for your gas as well as mine?" He said that was only fair. "Why? Why is it fair that I pay for your gas? I have my own to deal with. And what if you lose your job and you can't make the payments? Did that ever occur to you?"

"You just don't know how this works is all. You pay for both our gas and half the truck payment. That way I don't lose my truck and you don't lose your house. It'll work out, you'll see." She growled at him, something that told him she was really upset with him. "Hudson, have I ever steered you wrong before?"

"Yes, every single time you open your mouth and say, 'I got us a plan.'"

Well that had hurt him too, and he'd left her standing there. Then things had gone wrong after that. He'd had to skedaddle out of town quick, leaving her hanging out to dry.

But he was coming home now, and they'd be all right. She never could hold a grudge against her old man. Smiling, Burt decided that he was going to like her new husband even if it killed him a little. And if he gave him too much trouble? Well, Burt had ways of dealing with that kind of thing too.

CHAPTER 6

The castle was beautiful. They'd only seen the outside of it, but Emma could easily see herself living there for the rest of her life. It did need some repairs, she could see a few things that needed to be fixed, but the drawbridge and the actual moat around it was more than she'd ever dreamed of.

As soon as they got out of the car the doors opened, and what she could only surmise was staff came pouring out of the building and stood in line. She asked Liam what was going on.

"They knew we were coming here and are trying to make a good impression, I guess. Mason said that most of them have been here for centuries." She looked at the staff and wondered if they were all vampires. "No, none of them are. It's something to do with working for him, and they live forever. I'm not sure how that works now that he wants to sell."

They got out of the car and the stern looking butler came to the front of the line. He looked like he could have bent nails with his look. Giggling a little at the thought, she smiled at him. He bowed, then stood, holding a little tray with a letter on it.

"I am Hawkins, Your Lordship. Lord Mason said I was to give you this first thing. Also, there is a group of men in the parlor, my lord, that wish to speak to you about the town proper. They are aware that you will need a few minutes to settle, so I hope you don't mind, but I served them tea." Liam took the envelope and said that was fine. "My lady, if you'd like to meet the staff, they're ready for you."

"Hmm, sure. Why not. But I don't think we'll be here that long." He nodded, but introduced her to the cook first, Mrs. Peach was her name. "Hello, and what a lovely name. I was wondering if while we're here, you could share your recipes? My sister-in-law is looking for a very good scone one. She loves to bake."

"Of course, my lady." Emma, what she was trying to remember to call herself, told her what she went by. "I cannot call you by your given name, my lady. It's not proper. But you may call me Peaches if you like. That's what the staff calls me."

The rest of the staff introduced themselves as she made her way down the line. She heard Liam talking to Hawkins, but ignored him for the moment. There was something very odd going on here.

They were acting like she was their new boss. And more than that, they were telling her, in detail, what they did in the castle, as well as where they lived when not working. All but one of them lived and worked right there. The one that didn't, a young lad by the name of Winston, lived in town with his momma. When she'd met them all, she found herself with Peaches as the rest went into the home.

"We're here to see to the castle and the town. I guess Mason told you we'd be coming?" Peaches said that they'd gotten a call, yes. "The town, do you think they have the funds to buy the land there? I mean, it's going to be tough, I think, for them, after all this time."

"I'm sorry, miss, but Lord Mason said that you'd take care of us. You're not going to sell the castle, are you?" Emma glanced at

Liam, then back at the cook again. She must have seen confusion on her face, because she smiled at her before continuing. "He didn't tell you, did he, miss?"

"I don't think so." Peaches nodded and wrapped her arm around her as they bypassed the rest of the staff, who filtered off throughout the castle. The short curtsy from some of the women might have been nice, but Emma was too confused to think about it for now. "We're not here to take pictures of the place to put it on the market, are we?"

"No, miss. I mean, you could sell it should you want, but Lord Mason told us that you were the new owners." She'd known the little shit had something up his sleeve when he sent them here. As the two of them entered the great kitchen, she turned to Peaches when she continued. "I'm sure that it'll all be sorted out."

"Oh, it will be. As soon as I get back home and stake him out to burn." She knew that she had shocked the elderly woman, but right now she was as pissed as she'd ever been. "What else is going on that you can tell me, please? And why did he do this to us?"

"He said that he hated this place. And he did. All his life. Why, the stories that I could tell you about his parents would make you angry...well, angrier than you are now. But they were not nice people. And the staff was glad that young Mason was able to cut ties with them." She asked where his parents were now. "Gone. We all felt it when they were taken care of. Lord Mason came back just after and told us we'd be safe, as he was going to own the castle. We never saw him but a few times after that. Not much, for sure. But he would send letters to us and made sure that we were paid well. He's a good man. I do hope you're not going to kill him, miss."

"I won't. I don't think." Peaches nodded as they sat in the

kitchen. Well, she sat, and Peaches rushed around the kitchen making tea and filling a plate with cookies and other baked goods. "What about the town?"

"Those men showed up about an hour ago. They don't seem to be happy about taking over the running of things. I know that some time ago there was an offer up for them to purchase it, but nothing ever came of it. I think that Lord Mason got himself busy with other things. But they're here to talk to you and the mister. You own the town as well." Emma had figured that out too. And when Liam joined her, he ate most of the cookies on the plate and drank a stout cup of plum tea before he spoke.

"This wasn't anything I knew about." She said that she knew that. "We own this place, ten thousand acres, as well as the town. He wants us to sell it to the people or kick them out. Mason seems to think that they're being lazy about making any sort of repairs and upgrades, getting fat off the money."

They both looked at Hawkins when he cleared his throat. "The schools were to be improved several years back. There was funding put in an account to do so, but it's all gone but for a little. To keep the account open, I was told. Lord Mason would put funds in there when they asked for it. A new truck for the city department. An addition to the hospital. I have an accounting of what Lord Mason put into the account that was sent to me this morning." Liam asked for it and Hawkins left. When he returned, he had a thick file. "I've been a part of this household for many years, my lord. And in doing so, I have seen a great many things going on. I started to keep track of it, all for myself, should Lord Mason return. This is the file that I was sent, but this one is my own accounting."

Liam looked over the one that Mason had sent while Emma looked at the thicker file. It dated back over seven hundred years.

Hawkins told her he'd only brought her the most recent file. That sent her head into a tizzy. Asking for the paperwork from the past five years, he showed her where to find it.

"If I read this right, it says that Mason has put over a hundred million into that account over the last seven years." She added quickly in her head, and said that was about right. "It was earmarked for the hospital expansion, a new high school, as well as a grade school. Were they built?"

"No, my lady. The hospital is on the verge of being shut down. The townspeople have been driving the extra miles to the city hospital because this one is so out of date. And we have more children being taken to the outer schools than stay right here in the town." Hawkins showed her the attendance records over the years, and there was a very steep decline, in students as well as teachers. "Yet the money allocated for teachers has never decreased. It's being spent on personal things. A new house has been put in for the town mayor. The wife of one of the town leaders goes on holiday several times a year and brings back many things. Nothing for her staff nor the town, but for herself. She and her friends, women like her, rich and spoiled, have lavish parties that sometimes the staff is not paid extra for doing." Emma looked at him. "I'm not spying, my lady, but this is my master's money they are spending."

"I'm just impressed, Hawkins. You could be a fine cop if you wanted to." She smiled at him when he flushed. "And these men, they're here now? All of them?"

"Yes, my lady. One was away, but when he was called in, he came back quickly enough. There is a jet for them that sits waiting for their use as well. As you can see there, it was purchased about the time the hospital was to be upgraded." Emma was going to murder these men. But first she thought it a good idea to talk to

Mason.

In minutes, he was standing in the kitchen with them. Liam had called out to him using their connection, and when he was told the few things that they'd found out, he came to them. He was pissed too. So much so that the staff had gone into hiding.

"You're scaring everyone." Mason glared at her and she laughed. "That might work on everyone here, but not me. You lied to us."

"I did no such thing. It was my intention to sell this place, but after some thought, I decided to make it a gift to you. And now I am glad that I have." She thanked him and kissed his cheek. "You are a good person, Emma. And I hope that we can get this cleared up soon so that you can enjoy the rest of your honeymoon."

With Hawkins and Peaches' help, he was brought up to speed. At one point, Mason asked why no one had told him, and Hawkins reminded him that he'd told him he wanted nothing to do with the place or the problems there.

"I am truly sorry, my good man. I should have.... This is my fault, and I shall fix it." Hawkins told him it was his pleasure to have served him all these years. "And mine to have you here watching out for me. I shall make this up to you today. You will need to help me, I think, you and the Harrisons. We will get them where it hurts. Their wallets filled with my money."

The plan was a good one. She wouldn't say it was perfect. Emma wanted to shoot the four men in the other room, but they told her that could be plan B. Walking in with Liam at her side, she smiled at the men. They were so in trouble right now.

~~~

Mason listened to the men explain to Liam why the money was spent elsewhere while he stayed out of sight. Liam brought up how the roads needed to be repaired, and that in coming into town today, he'd noticed that they were in poor shape while driving. One of the men swore that they'd had them repaired a few weeks back. When Liam asked for receipts for that, they told him that they'd lost them.

"Lost them? How is that possible? Never mind, for now. I'd like for you to take me to where the repairs were made." The men said nothing, but Mason knew what they were thinking. They thought that Liam was a stupid American and he'd believe anything they told him. "Also, I'd like an audit of the money in the town account. There is...let me see here, over one hundred million dollars missing."

"That went to other projects." Liam asked him what projects. Since Mason had no idea who was speaking, he called them one, two, and so on. One laughed. "Have you ever run a town, sir? I would explain it to you, the everyday costs of keeping things going, but you'd not understand. Lord Mason trusted us, and I do hope you do the same."

"Well, Mason isn't in here right now, is he? And I want an accounting." There was soft laughter, and Liam cleared his throat. "One hundred million dollars. Where is it? And I want to see receipts for each thing you spent it on."

"We don't have any. That would be just silly to hold onto things when Lord Mason never asked for them. You should take our word for it, sir. We've been doing this for a long time. We do know what we're about." This time he heard Emma laugh. "I'm sure you must have things to do, Lady Emma. If you would leave us to our business, we'll be done directly."

"You want the poor little housewife out of the way, do you?" Mason didn't hear an answer, so he assumed that the man nodded. "Well, tough shit, you little fucker. I want to know where that money is, and right now. Or would you like for me to go through your records? Let me see here, a boat was purchased by Roger Dumas just four months ago. There was a house built for Andrew Carson. Wow, how many kids do you have that you needed a twelve-bedroom home? There is mention of a jet, as well as a bowling alley. You actually used the school improvement funds to build a bowling alley? Why the fuck are you thinking that a bowling alley would educate your children?"

"Who told you that? Where did you get that information?" She laughed again and Two continued, all signs of humor gone now. "Those things were bought by the money that Lord Mason pays us monthly for our services. And as I told you, the money in that account went to other projects. You shouldn't be bothering with that, anyway. We know, as we've told you, what we're doing here."

"Really? From what I can see, you're doing a shitty job. As for your money, your paycheck is deposited in your accounts each month, not in the town's money. This was cash used. Which I'm sure if I asked, was all paid out right after a deposit was made into the account." That was Mason's cue to come in, but he paused just a moment to see where Liam would go with this. "Per the records I have, you were getting paid a great deal to make this town prosper and grow. But from what I've seen and been told, the only people prospering from this are the four of you. Tell me, why on earth should I continue to pay you when you've done nothing that you said you would? Or for that matter, why shouldn't I have you arrested for fraud and theft?"

"Lord Mason trusted us. We just assumed that you would as well. If not, then I think you'll have to find someone else to run this little town." Mason walked in to see them all standing, and he wanted to tell them to sit, but they stared at him as if they had no idea who he was. "I cannot wait until you try and find someone that has done as much as we have for everyone here, with the pitiful salary we were told to use. And if you think that this is a man to do it, then you'll be begging us to come back and continue on as we are now."

It was then that it occurred to him that he didn't know them anymore than they knew him. No wonder their voices didn't sound familiar. These were not the people that he'd left in charge of his town. Then it occurred to him that it had been several years, decades more than likely, and that was why he didn't know anyone. Sitting next to Emma, he asked her to introduce them to him.

"Well, the one standing next to the fireplace is Asshole. That one is Dumbass that is about to piss himself. The one in the chair is Dickhead. And the one standing up, still, is Fucktard." She winked at him. "They might have other names, but since we didn't care, I didn't bother remembering them. But if you ask me, the names I gave them are much more suited to their profiles."

"You will remember yourself, young lady." Mason leaned back in the seat when Liam did. Fucktard was about to get his ass handed to him, he'd bet anything. "We're upstanding members of the council that run this town for Lord Mason and his family. You'll do well to keep your tongue behind your teeth."

"You're an idiot, has anyone told you that before? And no, I don't think I'll keep my tongue behind my teeth. I might need them to tear your throat out, you little pisser. And you will remember yourself, you little shit. I'm in charge now, and if you ever talk to me that way again, I will kick the living shit out of you, then mop it up with your head. Sit down and shut the fuck up." Fucktard sat, but he looked ready to bounce back up again when she snapped her fingers. "Sit, damn it. I've tried to be nice, but you're really pissing me off."

Fucktard looked around, and Mason knew he was frustrated. He'd leave thinking that the couple with him would tire of this and allow him to continue his business of stealing from him. These men would soon figure out that they were dealing with the wrong...or he supposed the right, people.

"I think this has gone on long enough. I will come back when it's a better time for you, Mr...? I don't think I caught your name." Liam told him and introduced him to his wife, Emma. "And you, sir? I didn't catch your name either."

"Lord Mason; your bank, apparently." Fucktard sat down then, missing the couch entirely and landing on the floor. "Yes, I see that you remember your benefactor. Now, I should like to have your proper names, if you don't mind. That way when I tell the townspeople who has been stealing from them, I'll have the correct names. Because while they'll think that the names my daughter has given you are apt, they'll like the real names when they tar and feather you. When you leave here, if you do, then I would pack up the little that you own and get out of town, perhaps even the country."

"Lord Mason, you have to let us explain so that you can understand what has been going on." Mason told Dumbass that he did understand, better than they might think. "We were going to pay it all back when it became necessary for the projects to be done. We were...We were only borrowing it."

"Borrowing it? And just how did you think to pay it back? By leaving the country, as I suggested? Oh yes, I'm well aware of the offshore accounts that you have. As well as the homes that you've purchased with my money." He looked at his nails, then at the man, letting his fangs stretch in his mouth. "Your names."

The compulsion was hard to ignore. The first one to answer was Dumbass. His name, as it turned out, was Roger Dumas.

Dickhead was William Strouse the Ninth. Asshole was James Wilkins, and Fucktard was Andrew Carson. Mason turned to Hawkins when he entered the room. Quietly, he asked him if the wives of the men were here now, as he had requested. Hawkins told him that they were.

"Good. Show them in, please. And have the local constables shown up as well?" Hawkins told him that they, too, were in on the scams. "I see. Well, it looks as if I might have to clean house, don't you think?"

"Yes, my lord, it looks as if you might." Hawkins was glowing with happiness.

Mason glanced at Emma, knowing that she had the ability to see things that even he could not. When she grinned at him, Mason thought that he surely loved this woman, and did really think of her as his daughter, just as he did Liam as his son. She was one of the reasons that he'd done all this, for her.

The women, wives of these men, were shown in, and treated them with the same disrespect that their other halves had. Until, that is, he was introduced to them. They then threw not only their husbands under the bus, but anyone else that was thought of. These women, he'd bet, thought there wasn't any way he'd be able to throw them out. Not with them being the poor wives of such dastardly men. Their words, not his. When he'd heard about as much as he could stand, he asked Emma if she could quiet them down.

The shrill whistle that came from her mouth made him laugh. The room was so quiet then that he could hear the grandfather clock that stood in the hallway. Standing up, he paced the room several times. He knew what he was going to do, had known before entering this room, but he did like a good scare when he could get it.

"You'll sign not only your homes, but the contents, over to Liam and Emma." Carson stood up and sat back down when he stared at him. "As I was saying, your homes, contents, as well as any cars, boats, and any toys you might have purchased instead of using the money where it had been earmarked."

Liam cleared his throat and handed him a list. It was not just a list of the purchases each man had bought for himself, but the date and the amount paid for it. He asked Liam where he'd gotten this.

"Hawkins has been keeping an accounting for some years. He wanted to make sure that you were aware of things." He nodded. Mason was going to do something for the man, just as soon as this was over. He had, because of his loyalty to him, saved him a great deal of time. "You should look over the reports that Stormy is sending to us this morning. And the accounts are empty as of ten minutes ago...she moved it back to here. The offshore accounts are also emptied out, as well as she's found the money that has been stashed all over their properties. That still only accounts for about a quarter of what they used. Stormy has been very busy, I think."

Nodding, he turned to look at the four men and women. There was going to be a reckoning for them. Not only would they lose all that they had, he wanted them to pay with more than just the tangibles that they'd acquired. Then he thought of what they were going to do.

"Starting tomorrow morning, each of you will show up at the hospital and help empty bedpans, take out the trash, whatever they—"

"I will not." Carson stood up. "You can't make me. I will not subject myself to this sort of treatment. Do you have any idea who I am?"

Mason snapped his fingers and the man was lifted two feet from the floor. His wife started screaming, as did the other women, and Emma told them to shut the fuck up. When there was silence again, he looked at Carson.

"Do it or die. I think I will enjoy killing you. Children without proper care, teachers working under the conditions that you left them to. Roads that served no other purpose than to be there because of the holes and ruts in them. You have let this town run to near ruin, and I am going to do the same to you." Carson started sobbing. His pants were damp with urine when he set him back to his feet. "Starting tomorrow you will make restitutions, or I will return and you won't be able to hide from me. Do you understand?"

"Yes, but we meant no harm." Mason asked him what that was supposed to mean. "You left us here without any supervision. What did you expect us to do? I'll tell you what we did, we did what we had to, and that should have been enough for you. And now you're here making demands that we don't want to do. How are we supposed to carry on if you are making these demands on us and taking our money? You just can't do that to us. Not at all."

Telling Hawkins to show them to the door, he sat down. There was no dealing with Carson today. But Mason had a feeling that he'd have to return and take care of the man. And not in a way anyone was going to like.

"Where will they live?" Mason told Emma he didn't care. "Yes you do, or you would have killed him. Where do you want us to house them?"

"There once was a shelter here. They can go there. And I will pay them a little, so they can afford to eat. Will that suit you?" Emma hit him in the back of the head and he smiled at her. "Not many would dare do that...you are aware of that, are you not?"

"I'm your darling little girl. You'd not harm me. And don't be a shit. I was only asking because I know you care." He laughed, and Mason found he really enjoyed this woman. "And don't think we didn't notice that you had them sign over the houses to us. We have to talk about what you've done for us."

"Not today, my child. I am far too tired to get into it with you for now." He stood up. "I have a favor to ask. Would you see to it that Hawkins is well rewarded? He has done us a great service."

"I will." He nodded and told her and Liam he'd see them when they returned home. "I'm going to hire someone to take over the watching of the town, all right? I think that Hawkins will do a great job at it, but convincing him to do it might be an issue. I have faith that you can talk him into it, can you not?"

"Yes, I do believe you are correct. And I'll not bully him into it like someone I know would."

When he was home, he smiled again. This woman was going to be the death of him. Or she'd give him a reason to live. He thought that the latter might be the case.

CHAPTER 7

Liam moved through the undergrowth, careful where he put his paws. They'd been at this for a couple of hours, and Emma was getting good at hiding in plain sight as her cat. He could smell her, but the scent wasn't fresh. He paused when he felt her touch his mind.

I figured out something. Would you like to know what it is? He said that he would. *That heat thingy, I can now focus on it and I can tell who it is and that they might be armed.*

And how did you figure this out? I'm assuming that someone is on the property, and that you can see that they're armed. She said that she could. *Where are they, Emma? I don't want you hurt.*

They're not hunting tiger. Though I guess if I were to step in front of them, I'd be shot. He's hungry. And hunting for game. I'm going to let him hunt. Liam lay down and waited for the shot. And when it came, he asked her if she was all right. *Yes, of course I am. But the man has two small children with him. I think they're living in these woods, Liam. They smell...I don't mean a nasty smell, but I can smell that they're sick too.*

I'll have them found, and we'll help them if they need it. She told him they did. *Yes, but some people are a little leery of getting help, even if they need it.*

Well then, I'll talk to him. He wasn't sure how that would go, but told her all right. *Also, when they leave here, you'd better fulfill your promise and make me come more than a dozen times. I'm sick of being needy when all these things keep getting in the way.*

Yes, my lady. He moved toward her, careful not to show himself. When he found her, he lay down beside her until she told him the three were gone. Then he moved over her and let his cat have his way with her.

It wasn't a good kind of sex, more of a coupling of two animals. Her cat would bitch the entire time, but that was all right too. When he was his cat and she human, Liam knew that she enjoyed that much better. When Emma spoke, he couldn't believe they were thinking the same thing.

This is not nearly as much fun, nor as satisfying, as when he takes the real me. He laughed, Liam just couldn't help it. *Can you teach him about foreplay? Or even a little bit of romance?*

You're making him sad. She told him he was making her sad as well. *When he's had his way, I promise to make it up to you.*

You've said that before. He let his cat have his fun, then Liam told her to shift. "Now this is more like it."

His cat licked every part of her pussy, as well as her clit, her thigh, and her knee. She tasted of warm sunshine and afternoons spent on the beach. Liam loved this woman more than he did life.

"Liam, I'm coming." Her cream filled his mouth, her body bowed up as he lapped at her. Each time he touched her with his tongue, he heard her screaming out again and again. And when he took his body back, continuing to eat her like she was his feast, he tasted her dewy need like a bee did nectar from a flower.

Moving up her body, he swirled his tongue into her navel, knowing that she would come just from that. He nipped her hip, her ribs, and her breast. Suckling on the tip, Liam held his cock at her entrance and slid it over her heat. When she rolled her hips up to meet his, he slammed forward, bringing a scream from her lips that was like music to his ears.

He felt her tighten around him. Her body's small tremors, building up to come apart again, had him taking her harder, kissing her mouth, her throat, and anyplace he could touch her. Her nails dug into his back and he felt blood rush over his skin. When he looked into her eyes, knowing that they were both close to something monumental, he saw her there. Her cat was snarling at him to take her, mark her.

Biting her throat seemed necessary. He tasted her rich sweetness and swallowed quickly. And when she came, holding him so tightly to her, he cried out as well. His body didn't just come inside of his love, but seemed to become a part of her.

Dropping on top of her, Liam didn't even have the strength to roll over. He was drained. When she laughed a little, he asked her what was funny, but even his voice sounded slurred, exhausted.

"You killed me." He grinned and rolled over, taking her with him. "Christ, what got into you? Not that I'm complaining, but holy shit, Liam, that was fantastic."

"You told me I had to make it up to you." Emma kissed his chest, right where his heart was. "I love you as well, my heart."

"I don't think I can move to get dressed and back to the house." He held her and told her that it didn't matter for now. "We leave in the morning. Are you ready for that?"

"Yes and no. I think we've done about all we can here, apart from the man and his kids. Hawkins is going to report to us weekly on things. We've brought in a new police force, or whatever they call them here. The construction is started on the new school and the library, as well as a few other projects that have been neglected. We've been gone a week more than we planned. Not that it's a bad thing, but I miss home. And I know you do as well."

"Yes, I want to see our house. I know it was a mess when we left, and your dad has been sending us pictures. But I want to go home, don't you?" He told her he did, very much so. "We'll take care of the man and his family, make sure that everything is working out, and then leave. I need this. I know the house needs some work yet, but we can get things ready to move into it when it's done."

"I do too. And we can do that, love." He kissed her then and they got up to dress. Liam was still feeling a little off, drained. Smiling and nodding his agreement to her, he took her hand in his as they made their way back to the castle. "You have to admit, this is going to be a great place to come and get away from it all. I mean, who do you know that owns a castle with servants and an entire town?"

"No one. And you're right. Especially now that we have people in place that we can trust. I'm glad that we have our own plane too. As much stuff as we're taking back, I don't think we could afford to have it taken on a domestic plane. I think they charge you by the pound after two pieces." But, he pointed out, they'd had a great time. "Yes, it was a lot of fun. And I think that everyone is going to love what we found for them."

Liam went to the office as soon as they were back. He had a few things that couldn't be put off any longer. The working vacation that they'd had was wonderful, but he had to take care of some items. As he began opening emails, he felt Riordan touch him through their link.

I didn't want to let you know until you were ready to leave. He asked him what had happened. *Emma's dad is around. Not with us, but Eunice said she's seen him around town. We think that he's waiting on you guys to return. He arrived yesterday.*

Well, it's going to be good to get this over with, don't you think? Riordan said it would be, but it would also be hard on Emma. *I don't know. She's been talking about him for the last couple of days, and I think she knew he'd be showing up. Emma said that he'd come sniffing around for some money or to borrow something.*

Yeah, I thought of that too. I had the rig put in the barn and the locks changed on the truck and the barn. I don't know that he'd just take it, but with him, it's hard to judge. Liam thanked him. *Anyway, you're not going to believe your house now. Eunice, she pulled a lot of strings and it's nearly complete. I think she had four crews working on it at the same time. Even the yard is done.*

We were just talking about that today. How much we had yet to do before we could move in. His brother told him it was ready to move into. *Christ, that'll be wonderful. Can you do me a favor? Can you stock the fridge for us? You have no idea how exhausted we're going to be for the next few days, and it would be nice to have food in the house.*

Not only will that be done for you, but you have a staff as well. Eunice again. I don't think she's planning to live with you, but she has been at the house every day making sure that they're working. Not in a terrible way. She's been nice to the workers, as well as anyone that comes around. The other day she had a cookout for everyone. I like her, and the aunts do as well. Liam told him some of the things that Emma had told him about her aunt. *Good. I think she'll fit right in with the rest of the madness around here.*

Liam was just finishing up the last email to send out when Emma joined him. She sat down in the chair across from him, but said nothing. As he began the process of shutting down the computer, he thought of how much he loved this woman. And what he'd do to make her happy. When she sighed heavily, he asked her what was wrong.

"The man on the grounds? The one with the kids? He's the brother to Dumbass." He knew who she was talking about. And even though she knew all their names as well as he did, she continued to call them by the names she'd given them that first day. "Why would you have all that money and then just leave your own family out to dry? Well, I fixed him up."

"How did you fix him up? And which one?" She grinned. "Am I going to like this? Or am I going to have to delay our flight home so I can bail you out of jail?"

"First of all, the police love me. I don't think they'd arrest me even if I robbed a bank. Secondly, why do you assume I've done something wrong? I mean, I didn't, not really, but why assume the worst of me?" She came to him and sat on his lap. "Mr. Dumas is going back with us. So are his children. A little boy, Charlie, and a little girl, Jess. Anyway, he wants to start fresh where no one knows him. As you can imagine, his name means shit around here."

"I don't mind him going, but what will he do there?" She told him he was a teacher. "A teacher. Okay. Then why, other than his name being shit, was he hiding in our woods?"

"Dumbass thought it would be good if his brother was dead and he had to take on the children. You know, I really do hate these guys. Anyway, if he was dead then he could take on the kids and get more sympathy if or when Mason came around. I don't think they would have gotten any more care than the town did, do you?" He told her probably not. "I've talked to Storm, and she's going to make sure they have the paperwork they need to travel with us, as well as a position and a house when they get there. My dad is around too."

The change of subject so quickly didn't confuse him as much as it had before. He just took it in stride, much like he did her thinking pattern. Details might have been worked out in her head, but she didn't voice them unless asked. He told her what he knew.

"And Riordan changed the locks on the rig for you. He said your dad might not touch it, but he didn't want to take any chances." She said he'd more than likely take it and think she'd have no problems with it. "That's sort of what he thinks."

"Are we ready to go then?" He told her they were, but neither of them moved. "I'm going to miss being here. Can we make it a point to come here when we get a chance? I mean, like a couple of times a year?"

"I think we can arrange that." Liam told her how they'd gone to the mountains last year for Christmas. "Maybe we can convince them all to come here for the next one."

By noon they were on their way home. It was going to be a long ride, but it was made more enjoyable by the children. Jess was the youngest at six, and her older brother Charlie, at nine, tried to act like it was no big deal to be going to another country. Liam was glad to have Weston to talk to as well.

~~~

Emma wandered around the house. Liam had gone into town about an hour ago, and she'd been just going from room to room since he'd left. There was so much done and so much going on that she'd caught herself twice just staring at a room. Her aunt came into the room with her and smiled.

"Overwhelming?" Emma nodded. "Yes, I can see that. I'm thinking that since you were in that truck for so long, you'd kinda like the ability to stretch out your wings, so to speak."

They sat down on one of the nicest sofas that she'd ever felt. She knew that some of the things had been purchased a while ago by Liam. He'd been storing things for some time in the anticipation of buying this place. And if the rest of the furniture was like this, she was never leaving the house again.

"I guess you know that Dad is around. I've not seen him yet, have you?" Aunt Eunice said she'd not had the displeasure of talking to him yet, but she had seen him from a distance. "Yes, I guess he would know that you're here. By the way, you're moving in here with us. I know you like to go at your own pace and travel, but I'd very much like for you to consider this your home base."

"I don't want to intrude." Emma could hear the hint of excitement in her voice. "Besides, I have a realtor that is looking into a house I've been thinking about purchasing. I'll just make that work."

"I don't know if you understood me or not. I didn't ask. I said you were." She leaned back on the other couch. "Dad isn't going to be welcome here, if that's what is holding you back. I'm not going to be able to forgive him for what he did to me. And how much he's done to me in the past. I've been thinking a great deal about things, him and my relationship with him, and he wasn't a good father, nor a good man. He's a lazy fuck that needs to have his ass handed to him on a dirty platter."

"That sounds like an excellent plan. He hurt you. I wondered how long it would take you before you set him on his ear. That man was always the most selfish man I ever knew. Even as a kid." She looked upset for a few moments before continuing. "Honey, did you know that your mother is alive?"

"Yes, I even know where she is." Aunt Eunice nodded and said she'd figured she might. "I didn't find her. I mean, it was never in my mind to do that, but Stormy did. She's my sister-in-law, and I'm sure you've talked to her. Anyway, she said that she was looking into things about my dad and come across her name.

96

And the only reason she looked was to see if she had anything to do with what Dad did to me."

"She didn't." Emma said she knew that. "Your mom, she tried her best with your dad. He just wasn't the right man for her. I mean, she loved you to pieces, but he wouldn't allow her to take you. I think he just wanted to have something she didn't. But it nearly broke her, leaving you behind. But Burt, he didn't give her much of a choice. She left with nothing but the clothing on her back. Much like he's done to you recently."

"She's happily remarried with two other children. I'm not going to bother her now. I mean, if she wanted to I'd love to see her, but it's been too long for both of us now." Aunt Eunice nodded then handed her a sheet of paper. "What's this?"

"Her address and phone number. She told me to give it to you if you weren't too mad at her for leaving you. And her husband and children know about you. They've been keeping up with you through me. I'd send her notes, as well as pictures of you when I got them. And she was happy to get them. It nearly broke her heart when she found out he'd hurt you." Emma looked at the address and thought of how far her mom had run to get away from her dad. "Burt took her for a ride too. When she married your dad, she was going to have you. It wasn't a storybook romance, nor a good start to a marriage for either of them. Nora came from money, and Burt lost nearly every penny of it just before you were born. By the time you came along, they were living in a car. It wasn't until she called her daddy to help her that she had to leave Burt or be broke again. And I don't mean financially, either."

"When Dad and I started driving together, I wanted to believe that he'd changed. That he'd gotten his life straightened out and was making good on some things. I had no idea that he'd lost his house due to some unfinished scams, and that he'd lost his job by arguing with the boss over what he thought was a better way of doing things. He even thought I could cut some corners when I made some drops, tried to convince me that no one would care. I wanted to be good at my job, not have people wonder what I was going to steal from them next. I guess I wanted to believe that he was going to not take me for everything I had worked hard for." Aunt Eunice just nodded. "When he bought the rig, I was terrified at what he'd done to get it. Who he'd promised something that I was going to be caught up in. I never dreamed that he'd sign my name to a loan, using my house as the down payment."

"When we were younger, for my birthday I was given money by our grandmother. She'd not been able to go shopping, she'd told me, and gave me cash. It was a big deal for me to have cash instead of a gift for me. It meant I had the freedom to purchase what I wanted. And I wanted it to be special." Emma knew her dad had ruined it for her. "After about three months of deciding, I was going to get tickets to the movie theater for Burt and me. And pay for treats when it was over. I was so excited to be able to share it with him. But when the day came, I told Burt about it and he told me to give him his share of the money and he'd call it even. Call it even. I told him how there wasn't any even involved, it was my money. He slapped me, then took half my birthday money, and told me I was going to use it on him anyway, and he'd rather have the cash than to spend time with me. I think right then I was finished trying to be his sister. After that, I never trusted him again."

"Oh, Aunt Eunice. I'm so sorry." She waved her off, but Emma went to sit with her anyway. "I'm not going to be getting the daughter of the year award when he gets here. I'm only telling you that so you can close your ears when he does. I've had enough of him and his scams."

"You do it, honey. If you don't, he'll hurt you in ways that he'll only think you did to yourself. I know that." Emma had figured that out as well. "Don't you lend him a dime, either. There isn't any way for him to pay you back, even if he thought he might."

"He's going to prison." Aunt Eunice asked her for what. "I found out that he's been selling off loads. Three since he left me, and about a dozen before that. He took loads and sold the goods from them instead of taking them to the drop location. That's a federal offense, because he did it over state lines."

"Well, good." Emma laughed. "He might be able to find him some work that won't hurt either of us in that place. Might even find himself a boyfriend or two. I don't think they'll take too kindly to the way your dad does business while in that place, do you?"

"No, I think he'll pay for any scams he tries out in there, and pay dearly." Aunt Eunice nodded. "Now, we're going to settle this house up, then be a family. Liam and I really do want you to stay here with us. I promise, I'll never ask you what you're doing, nor will I be the overbearing niece. Come and live with us, Aunt Eunice."

"Thank you." She asked her aunt for what. "For being a good girl. For taking this old woman into your home. And most importantly, for not being your father. You have no idea how good that makes me feel."

For the rest of the afternoon and well into the evening, they went from room to room making a list for each on what was still needed. Mostly it was furniture, but there were other things as well. Such as frames for pictures, linens for the three extra bathrooms, and her aunt's rooms needed to have her things moved into them.

Aunt Eunice was taking a suite of rooms, which would include her having a living room, a bath, as well as a bedroom that was as big as her entire house had been. Her aunt was happy beyond words.

They decided to meet Liam in town to have dinner with him, and his parents were going too.

"That lovely woman, Andi, is going to have a baby soon. I just love all the women in your family, Liam. You're a very lucky man." He told her he was, and kissed Aunt Eunice on her cheek. "You're a flirt, does your wife know that?"

"She does, and loves me all the more for it. I'm glad that you're moving in with us, Aunt Eunice. It'll be wonderful having two of the most beautiful women I know around." She blushed brightly. "And when you travel, you always know that you have a family that loves you, including my family, and a place to call home."

Dinner was fun. Aunt Eunice decided she wanted pizza, and that was where they went. They also, with the help of Liam's mom, did some shopping online for things that the house needed but could wait for. And Liam made arrangements to get her aunt's things to the house. All in all, it was an amazing evening. Tomorrow was going to be hard in comparison. Emma was going to find her dad and see what he wanted from her. It was time to get this finished, she thought.

CHAPTER 8

The paperwork was being filed now and it was out of his hands. Liam was glad to have this part of it over with. As he made his final notes on his computer, he thought of the millions of dollars' worth of merchandise that had been stolen from the companies that trusted to have them delivered. Burt Hudson was going to go down for a lot of theft.

His dad walked in his office just as he was hitting send on his email.

"I got me a favor." He told him anything. "You say that now, but I'm thinking that you might change your mind before I get finished. It's about this building that is going in downtown."

"Which one? Last month there were four going out of business, and I was downtown last night and I could see where six were going in. You've been busy." He nodded, but Liam could see he was distracted. "What's going on, Dad?"

"I was thinking that I might have messed up a bit. Not a great deal, but a little. I'm thinking that the clothing business that is going in, it's not on the up and up." Liam asked him why not. "Well, you know a few years ago, when that company went and did a lot of logos for the colleges around without their permission? I think that's what is going on here. They have some college sweatshirts in the window. There are also things like glasses and book bags like the kids carry. And when I looked them up online, they're nearly double in price for what this place is selling them for in the store. They're cheating somebody and I know it. I don't want to look bad to any college. How do I check it out?"

"Are you invested in the company?" He told him only in that he owned the building. "Okay, I'll make a few calls and see what I can find out for you. If they don't have a license to sell those things, it won't come back on you unless you knew it when they went in."

"No, all the contract says is a clothing store. New stuff, not used. We got one of them going in too, by the way. Secondhand Anns, it's called. Baby stuff and things like that." Liam asked Dad how many other things he had going. "Here and there. I got this man calling me from New York that wants to come and talk to me about some of the buildings we own as a family. I told him to talk to one of you boys. He might call, I don't know which one of you. And we're having a fundraiser for the new community building that Aedan is working on. There are other projects too, but I don't have a lot to do with them."

Liam would bet his last nickel that not only was his dad involved in them, but overseeing a few of them too. His dad was smart, and Liam was proud of him and the rest of his family. He put a search in his computer about licensing and came up with the same thing his dad had been talking about. It carried a hefty penalty if they were doing this without permission.

"What are you two up to?" Aunt Eunice came into the room with a smile on her face. "You, Mr. Harrison, look like you might have had something cooking and it's working your way."

"Nah, just looking into a few things. I hear tell you ladies are going to have a shindig tonight. Baby showers sure ain't what they used to be. I'm glad that you're going too. I think I can say for the entire family that we're glad you're around."

"Thank you. It's nice having family near you, isn't it?" She asked what they were into.

"We're trying to revitalize the downtown area. Aedan, my son, he's hoping that with this town as a model, he could get some others to do the same. We've owned a few of the buildings in the area for some time now, and it's good to see someone using them instead of them sitting empty."

"Emma said that the school is being worked on as well. I used to be a teacher back before the world became too fast for me, and I have to tell you, nothing like going into a fresh room and making it sing for you." Dad told her they were making up a fund for each room too. That way the teachers wouldn't have to put out their own money. "That's wonderful. Oh, how nice. You let me know what you need in that department, and I'll surely help. You doing anything like raffles and such?"

"No, Bri, she's in charge of that with the girls. She was thinking that we could do some bake sales. Also, garage sales where people donate some of their junk to sell off. Bri is good at telling people they want to help with this." Dad looked around as if he was afraid Mom might have overheard him. "My wife, she'd be the one to talk to if you really want to help her."

"I think I will. Thank you, Ordan." Dad nodded. When his cell phone rang, he went to the hall to answer it and Eunice looked at Liam. "What do you need for me to do?"

"Do? I'm not sure what you mean." She asked him what he needed her to do about Burt. "Oh, to be honest with you, Emma hasn't wanted to talk about it. She did say after thinking about it that she'd wait on him to come to her. I can't believe he's ballsy enough to come here knowing what he did to her. Not to mention you."

"He more than likely thinks she'd never be upset with him after all this time. He sort of thinks people love him despite him being a prick." Liam laughed. "Not that he thinks he's a prick, mind you. Burt isn't stupid either. He just thinks that things should go his way, no matter what. And he needs to be the center of attention. You going to help her?"

"No, I mean, I want to, but she has to do this on her own. Mom said she needed to know him for what he is. Not that I don't think she already does, but Mom thinks if I take care of this, he'll not take it to heart as much as he will with Emma doing it." Eunice said that was more than likely correct. "It's going to hurt her."

"Yes, more so than he has already. But to Burt, it'll be nothing to worry over. And he'll think that in a few weeks, less if he can hound her to death, she'll forgive and forget. I've been meaning to ask you. Do you think he'll hurt her physically?" Liam told her he'd better not try. "Because you'll kill him?"

"No, I won't, but she might. She's a good deal stronger than she was before he did that to her. Both mentally and physically. I'm thinking that if he tries anything like that, she'll take him down as her cat. He won't know that she is one and will push her too far. More so than he has already." Eunice nodded, but didn't look convinced. "What is it you know? You know something, don't you?"

"He's going to try and take her, I think, to get back at her. He'll think that holding her for ransom will get him what he wants, and that Emma will understand. I'm not positive that he'll go that far, but you should be prepared for just about anything concerning my brother. Burt will use him being her father to make her see reason." Liam asked her how he thought she'd understand. "Because what Burt wants, he gets. No matter what is happening to get it for him."

"He hurt you, didn't he? More so than just your birthday money you told Emma about." She didn't look as if she might answer, but she finally nodded. "Can you tell me? I won't tell Emma if you don't want her to know."

She sat in the chair and looked around. When she seemed to have herself prepared, the only way he could describe what seemed to be going through her mind, she looked at him. There was such sadness there that he found himself regretting asking her about it.

"I'd been married about a month. Emma knows that I was, but not why things.... Alex was so wonderful to me. And he even tolerated my brother and his ways about him. More so than I wanted to. But Burt didn't like me being married. He said that I was never there for him. While I did try to help him at times, he was so demanding. And Alex and I were so happy that I did find myself avoiding Burt in favor of my husband. Alex and I, we were so in love." Liam watched as she wiped at the tears on her face that streamed down her cheeks. "Alex had money. And in turn, I guess I did as well. Burt thought that since I had it, he had it. I know that I should have warned Emma about his tendency to take what he wanted, but he loved his little girl, I thought, so I didn't."

"She might not have believed you." Eunice nodded. "What did he take from you, Eunice? Your money?"

"Yes, but something much more important to me. He took my love. My husband." He waited for her to continue, but she cried softly for several minutes before she did. "Alex was out in the yard, directing the gardeners in the rose gardens for the upcoming party we were having. Burt hadn't been invited simply because it was business guests, not family. And no matter how many times I told him that, he was upset. Then.... He killed him with a rifle that he'd taken from Alex the month before. He'd borrowed it, much like he does everything. Borrowing without any intentions of bringing it back. We knew that he had, but never dreamed that he'd use it against my Alex. Burt killed him and told everyone it was an accident. But I knew. I knew he'd done it to try his best to get me in a position where he was first in my life again."

"He didn't go to prison for it." Eunice shook her head. "They believed that he'd done it by accident then?"

"Yes, oh, yes. You'll see when you talk to him, he can be quite convincing when he needs to be. I'm betting that he'll start on you first, then your family, before he tries to get Emma to give him something. But it won't be enough...whatever he wants, there will always be something else he needs or thinks he needs from her. Why he's not called you yet is beyond me. But he will. Someone in your family will get a call or a visit from him." Liam said that his family was well aware of the man. "Yes, I thought I was as well, but it did me little good, did it? I was left alone, with a hole in my heart as big as the world, and he'd done it. And gotten away with it."

Liam decided it was time to have a family meeting. He wanted his family to be aware of what he'd found out, as well as how far things were going with the theft of the merchandise from Whites as well as a dozen or so other companies that Burt had done business with. The shit, as they say, was about to hit the fan for the man, and Liam was glad that he was going to be there when it did. Picking up the phone, he knew just who to call.

"Mom, I need a huge favor." She told him he could have anything. "I need for you to call a family meeting, where we're all there and ready to plan. Burt is going to hurt my mate, and I want to be able to prevent that as best we can."

"They'll all be here at five-thirty, son, or I'll know the reason why." Liam thanked her. "Is it bad? Is he going to be really bad about this?"

"Mom, I certainly hope so. The man has terrorized enough people for several lifetimes." When he put the phone down, he knew they'd all be there. Mom could be pretty persuasive when she wanted to be.

~~~

Burt wasn't sure what he was going to do about all this work it was costing him to get to see his little girl. 'Course, he'd not tried all that hard to actually see her, but he had been trying to see her in-laws, while avoiding Eunice.

She was gonna be really upset with him when she found out that he was in town and bothering Hudson again. Well, he had news for her. He'd not done a darn thing yet. And he could talk to her when he wanted. He and his little girl had the best of relationships, and he was glad that she'd done so well for the two of them.

The man that came out of the office building where he'd been told the Harrisons were made him think he'd just wait until someone littler came out. This guy looked like he could lift up him and his truck. And he was as old as the trees. But he stopped walking and stared right at him, as if he had been waiting on him.

"You looking for someone, Burt?" He nodded at the man. And it occurred to him that he knew who he was. "Yeah, we know who you are and how you're related to my daughter-in-law. You tell me what it is you think I need to know, and I'll think about telling her. I probably won't, just so you know. I think you've done enough to poor Emma."

"Who?" He told him his daughter. "Oh yeah. I forget sometimes that she has a different name than Hudson. You don't want to be calling her that to her face. She gets powerfully mad about it. Just trying to keep you out of hot water with her. She's got herself a temper at times. I was wondering if you could do me a favor."

"No, I don't want to do you a favor. Not now, not ever. As for her having a temper? I haven't seen it except when we talk about you, which isn't all that often. But we all call her Emma. She told us to." That was strange. Whenever someone called her that when she was little, she'd bite their head off. "You never said why you were here. And if it was only for me to do you a favor, then the answer is still no."

"I was just coming around, letting the family know that I'm in town and all. I was going to go out and see her and that new husband of hers. Since I didn't get my invite to the wedding, I've been thinking it might have gotten shuffled around in the mail. She'd not want me to miss something so important as her getting married. But I've been running into some money troubles." The man only stared at him. "I could go out there if I had me a car or some cash to take out a cab. But I don't have it."

"There isn't a cab service in this town. You could try just outright buying you a car, but if you don't have a job or money, that won't work for you either." The man was dense, he thought. Burt wondered if he was addled with all them drugs he was taking to make himself look like the broad side of a barn. He knew there wasn't any way this man was this muscled without something helping him along. "Walking never hurt anybody. You could do that."

"Nah, I don't care much for walking any more than I have to. I was thinking that if you were going out there some time, I could hitch a ride with you. Or one of the others. I've been wanting to see her." The man said he wasn't going to see her until tomorrow. "Well, that'll work for me. I could meet you someplace."

"No." Burt waited for him to tell him why he wasn't going to take him out to see his only child, but the man just looked behind him again. "I have me some work to get done. If there is nothing else, I'll be moving along. And I'd suggest you do the same. Emma is happy, more than you ever made her. Just go back to where you came from."

The man just left him there, like he wasn't in the middle of a conversation with him. Darn it to heck fire. That wasn't polite. When the door opened again, he saw another big man and knew he was related to the older one. The rude one. Putting out his hand, Burt tried to put his best foot forward this time. He needed to get some walking around money, and nobody was seeing things his way.

"I'm Burt Hudson. My daughter is married to someone in your family, I'm thinking." The man stopped, but didn't take his hand. "You Harrisons, you're not too friendly, are you? That older man that just come out of that place, he is the rudest person I've met here. He an uncle of yours or something?"

"That was my father. And we're very friendly, but not to men who take advantage of their children." He asked him what he was talking about. "Leaving Emma high and dry after her losing her house and car for something you lied about. There is a long list of things I could go over with you, but I'm not going to. It's not worth me wasting my time over it."

"Oh, that was just a misunderstanding on her part. She knew I was wanting a new truck. And I knew that her house would work out just fine for the down payment and all. She just didn't get to the bank before I did. It's all fine now." The man said nothing. Burt didn't like them thinking he had to explain himself to these people. She was his daughter, and that's all they needed to worry about. "I was wondering if I could get to know you all before I go out and see her and that new hubby of hers. That other man, your daddy, he didn't have time to discuss the times and such that I could meet up with you. I was thinking that if I could get in good with you all, then she'd be all right with a few ideas that I have. I heard tell she's gonna sell off her truck. I'm gonna have to go and see her before she does a fool thing like that. I might have some uses for it."

"I believe someone is buying it tomorrow." Well, that wasn't going to work for him, and he told the man that. He told him again how he had some plans for it. "Why is it any of your concern if she sells her truck or not? I'm sure that she owns it. You have nothing to do with the sale. And if she does sell it, that money will be hers to do with as she pleases as well. Nothing to do with you."

"Sure it does. She's my little girl." Burt wasn't mad, he was frustrated. Smiling at the man, he decided to explain things to him. "I was going to use it, like I already said. You know, rent it from her. Not that I think she'd charge her old man for the use of something that she ain't using anymore, but I need to get back up on my feet. Then when I'm home, I can hang out with her, just me and her. You can understand that, can't you?"

"It's doubtful that anyone would want to willingly hang out with you, Burt. Besides, you don't have a CDL any longer. So, you buying the truck wouldn't do you any good. Or renting it. Either way, I'm sure you don't have the funds for either of those ideas." He seemed to know a lot about him. "I also think there are pending charges against you for forging her name to documents that you used at the bank. If you go and try to get that taken care of, your license I mean, someone is going to ask you about that part as well."

"Look here. Me and my *daughter*…," Burt made sure that he understood it was his daughter, "We got us an understanding about all this. I'm sure that she's sorry as ever that she put them cops out there to look for me, and I'm sorry that I didn't tell her after I used her place for my loan. We're good, you'll see it. And if the rest of your family is thinking that I done her wrong somehow, then us all getting together before I talk to her will be better. Don't you think? I mean, I could come to your house for a little dinner. I can come over any night. Someone would have to come and get me…I don't have the funds for a car just yet. Unless you want to buy me one. That way I can get around and not have to bother anyone for a lift now and again."

"No." He was having that said to him a lot today, and he was getting mighty mad about it. "You're not going to try and hang her out to dry again. You're not going to borrow money with no intention of paying it back. And you're definitely not going to get with my family and case the house so that you can come back and rob us blind."

"What a thing to say. My daughter isn't going to like you talking to me that way. She and I, we're real tight. Whoever you are, you're going to regret that. Who are you anyway?" He told him he was her husband. "Husband, huh? Well, that don't make it any better that you're being right rude to me. I want you to tell Hudson, my daughter, that I'm looking for her, and if she'd be so kind as to meet me someplace, I'd surely appreciate it. And don't think I'm not going to tell her how her dear husband treated me. Rude is what you are, just a rude man, and she's not going to take it kindly that you are."

Burt walked away. It was that or get the crap beat out of him.

He'd like to hit the younger man, but Burt wasn't stupid. He could tell that the man, her husband of all things, wasn't one to tangle with. Maybe he'd just tell her that he hit him. Emma sure wouldn't like her new husband beating on her daddy. He'd have to think of a way to get her to see that he'd been hurt.

As he made his way back to the little dive he'd been staying in, he had to route around to the window that he'd left open in the back. The owner was demanding that he pay him some of the money that he owed him. Burt just didn't have it yet, and the man wasn't going to call up Emma and tell her he needed it like he told him to do several times. She was going to be upset, he knew, with all the things that had been done to him since he'd been in this little town. He needed to start making a list with names. Then she could take care of them for him. People were just not as nice as they used to be.

Sliding in the window, he screamed when he saw someone sitting on the bed. He nearly wept with relief when he saw who was there.

"Eunice, you darn near scared ten years off my life. Who let you in here?" She didn't answer him, but she sure was giving him the evil eye. "I was going to go and see you later today. I heard that you were in town. Saw you got to go to the wedding too. I might have misplaced my invite or something. The mail ain't what it used to be, is it? Wasn't fair of them to not wait on me when my only child was—"

"You weren't invited and you know it. Not after what you'd done to Emma. I can't believe you'd think you would be." He sat down in the chair across from her, thinking that his little sister was looking mighty old nowadays. "Why are you here, Burt? You can't think that she's going to forgive you for what you did. Not to mention, you're still in hot water over that mess you made about things after she helped you out by taking you on some trips with her."

"I know she'll forgive me. She's my little darling and she loves me. And all that stuff from before? It don't mean a hill of beans now. Hudson is a good girl, and she'll take me back no matter what she thinks I done to her." Eunice snorted at him. "Now, don't be that way, Sis. You know as well as I that the bond between daughter and dad is unbreakable. She loves me too much to be holding that over my head. Besides, it's all been taken care of. There isn't anything wrong now. She paid everything off, and even though it was wrong of her to send them police after me, she won't let them take me away. Not with her having all that money."

"Only you would think that, Burt. Only you. But it's not all taken care of. You took her home, her money, and you had her life looked into like she'd been involved with you." Burt just waved her off. It was done, why did she have to keep harping on this? "What is it you're hoping that she's going to do for you? Give you money?"

"Yes, well, I'm hoping that she'll give me a place to stay, too. I saw that her husband has some money. And being her dad, she'd want me taken care of, don't you think?" She told him she didn't. "You always did hate me, Sis. Why is that? What did I ever do to you? You should have had more respect for me, me being your big brother and all. What is it you have in your head that I did to upset you?"

"You killed my Alex." He just shook his head. She never could get that out of her head, no matter how many times he told her to forget it because it was done. "You murdered him and we both know it. You didn't like that he was mine, so you took him from me."

"He's gone. Why do you always bring up stuff that's done and dealt with? For heaven's sake, I told you a million times, it was an accident. And if you want to know the truth, I thought you'd be grateful for that accident too." She asked him why he would think that. "Well, you got all that money, didn't you? Which you never shared with the one who made sure you got it. And you got to see me more. He was in the way, and needed to be gone, Eunice. I never did it on purpose, so you know, but I'm not unhappy that it happened like it did."

She stood up and so did he. Eunice could be a bear when things didn't go right. He hadn't a clue what she might have thought he'd done now, but he wasn't going to let her hurt him. Then he remembered the husband and stuck out his chin for her to hit. Whoever hit him would be all right if it got him to his daughter.

"I'm not going to hit you, Burt." He pouted at her. "You're going to be sorry that you came here. And sorrier yet that you did anything to Emma. She's not the child you left all those months ago. But a strong, loved woman that has figured you out."

"She's the only sane one around here, I'm thinking. That husband of hers, he's not a nice person either. Wouldn't even invite me to his home. Claimed I was going to case the place like I was going to rob it." She asked him if he was planning that. "No, I won't have to if Hudson comes through for me. And she will. She's always been there for me, and will be after this is all settled. If she'd of just done what I asked her to do in the first place and gone to the bank with me, I'd not have had to resort to signing her name. This is, if you really think on it, all her fault anyway."

"My God, Burt, have you no shame at all? How the hell can you blame your stupidity on her?" He didn't understand why she was all upset about it, so he didn't answer. And he wasn't stupid. "I can't be around you when you're like this. I'm leaving here. And if you're smart, which I know that you're not, you'll leave town and forget you even had a child. She will grind you in the dirt this time."

She moved to the door and he stopped her. "I sure could use some money, Eunice. Just whatever cash you have on you will be fine. And my hotel isn't paid for either. Hudson will see to it, but for now I'm having to come in the back way so I can't see the owner none." Eunice just stared at him. "Come on. I know you have it. You always have cash on you. I'll have Hudson pay you back when I go see her. And money will get me there quicker. Just whatever you have."

"I don't have anything for you." He reached for her purse and she snatched it back like she had extra strength or something. "What do you think you're doing? Were you going to rob me, Burt? Take my money when I told you no?"

"It's not robbing. It's borrowing until Hudson pays you back. Why do you have to make mountains out of mole hills? Just give me the cash and I'll have her pay you back. That's all I'm asking for." She pulled her purse to her chest and he shook his head. "Come on, Eunice. You know she's good for it. You've seen the kind of stuff that family has. Just the cash. I don't want to have to mess with the cards just yet. The room is costing her forty dollars a night, and I've been here for three days. Just pay that too on your way out."

He put out his hand. She'd give in, she always did. Well, not lately, but she had to be over that too. Her husband left her well off, and he'd not gotten anything from his part in her getting it. Burt was thinking of where he was going to have dinner tonight after she gave him some money when the door slammed. He was still standing there with his hand out, his empty hand out, when he realized that she'd left him.

"What on earth is wrong with everyone today? Like they don't know that I'm good for it or something." He'd talk to Hudson about this. She'd fix him right up. Yes, siree, she'd fix him in style. She was his little girl, after all. "Now what the heck am I supposed to do about getting me some dinner? And here I was thinking steak and a big fat potato. Darned people are really messing things up for me."

CHAPTER 9

Liam was working in the barn, looking to see how he could store more stuff in it when the new stuff arrived, when he heard someone shouting. Turning to look at Mac, he was going to him when his brother jumped. Asking him what was going on, Mac shouted again.

"She's in labor." It took Liam a second or two to realize what he'd said. "She's going to the hospital. Emma was there with her when her water broke. We're going to have a baby."

When Mac dropped to his knees, he did go to him then. He was pale, his face was clammy. Worried that he'd gotten too much sun, he waved him with his hand until he said he was all right.

"Christ, are you trying to have a fucking heart attack before the baby gets here? Shit, Mac." Mac just looked up at him. "What's going on? Tell me. Did she have an accident? Are they all right?"

"I'm going to be a dad." He said that was how it worked. "No, I mean, I'm going to be a father, and I don't have a clue what the hell I'm doing."

He smacked him in the back of the head and made his way to his car. Mac going to be a father was the least of his troubles if he was going to get all weird when there was news about the kid. He was in the car with it running when Mac got in the other side. As they pulled out of the drive, Mac started talking a mile a minute.

"She's going to be in a lot of pain, I'm betting. The childbirth teacher said she would. I know that she's really strong, but she'll be hurting. And then we'll be parents." Liam told him there might be a few minutes in-between there. "Be serious. I'm going to be a dad, and I'm afraid of fucking it up."

"You won't." He asked him how he was so sure. "Because you're a good man, and you have Dad and Mom there to keep you from fucking up too much. And I'm pretty sure that Andi won't let you hurt any of them."

"Yeah, there is that. Can you drive any faster?" Liam didn't press any harder on the pedal, thinking that late was better than not getting there at all. "Andi wants to make sure that our kids know that we love them. And that we'll always be there for them too. You're not driving faster."

"No, I'm not. And you will be there for them. And if not you, the rest of us will be whenever you need us to be. They'll know you love them too. I have no doubt about that." He nodded and asked about the speed. "You want to arrive at the hospital in one piece or not? I don't want to hear from Mom and Dad how stupid you were for making me wreck the car because you were impatient."

They arrived at the hospital ten minutes after Emma and Andi did. His family, all of them, arrived twenty minutes after that. Even Eunice and the aunts, Sally and Lynn, were there. This was family, he thought. Sitting down to wait after Mac left to find his wife, he held Emma in his arms. Ennis was going to check on Andi's progress and see what he could find out.

"She was so calm. Like she'd done this a thousand times

before." He told Emma about Mac. "She said that he'd been too calm about all this, and she fully expects him to lose it once she goes into hard labor. I guess she was right on that one. Andi said she's been practicing her stern look to keep him grounded."

"Andi is amazing. I think that when she has this baby, she'll want to go home and cook for us all. By the way, I've had someone go and get her brother so he could be here. He's been really excited about the baby too." Emma said that was very nice of him. "Nah, it's family. Speaking of which, have you heard from your dad yet?"

"No, and I don't care if he never contacts me. I know he will, but I can wait. I guess Aunt Eunice went to see him yesterday and it didn't go any better than his meet up with you. He's such an ass." He nodded. "Liam, let's have a child soon. Would you like that?"

"Yes, lots of them. But I want us both, especially you, to be ready for having a child." She looked up at him. "Do you want one now? I mean, even if it's only just the one, I'd be happy. Or several dozen. Whatever you want to do. It is your body, after all."

"I want a few, not a dozen. And it is my body, but I have no idea how this will work." He asked her what she meant. "Well, I know that I have a human baby and that it'll change later. I don't know when or what happens to trigger it. Because I'm a changed tiger, will that affect how its life will be? Do I have to do anything different than a human would have—?"

He put his hand over her mouth. "Slow down, babe. You're going too fast for me to answer. Okay, yes, you have a human baby, just as you would if you were a pureblood. When our child reaches fifteen or so it'll be able to feel its tiger, but not shift yet. They do sometimes, but not often at that age. It will depend on the cat and the person. As far as you being a changed tiger rather than a pureblood, yes, it will affect any children that we have. They could be a pureblood or half, like you. Or they might not be a tiger at all. They'll still have abilities, like they can heal faster, live longer, and all that, but not shift. Sometimes, but not often, if we were both changed tigers, then the odds would be more against them in all those areas." She asked about her doing anything. "You'd have to eat more red meat. Not like raw, but just red. You burn a lot of calories now; while pregnant you'll burn more. You've seen Andi snacking all the time. That's why."

Ennis came back to tell them that Andi was fine and that Mac was doing much better. Relieved that he wasn't going to faint, they all settled down to wait. He was excited as hell to become an uncle. He was sure that his excitement was only a fraction of how excited his parents were right now.

"When can we have a baby? I mean, we have a lot of sex. I remember something about being fertile, but I don't know how that works either." He explained it to her. "So, I have to be in heat for us to get that way. Okay. Is there a time frame that it happens in? Will I know?"

"Yes, to all those questions. And once you are, we'll have more sex than you can imagine." She looked at him hard. "I'm not kidding. The need to procreate is big, and we'll not be able to go out or anything once you are. All we'll want to do is touch, be touched, and have sex. Copious amounts of it."

"Why is it that I'm afraid to believe you?" He laughed when she smiled. "Why aren't any of the rest of them going to have a baby? I mean, Storm and Riordan have been married for a year now, right?"

"Yes, just about. But they're holding off until she is finished with a couple of assignments that she's doing for the president.

I think if you were to inhale deeply, you could tell that Nikki is going to have a baby. They both know, in case you were wondering, all of us know, but as they've not said anything yet, we haven't either." Emma asked about her. "No, you're not in heat, if that's what you mean. I'd know, and so would every male tiger around. Even the ones that aren't shifters."

"Really?" He told her yes. "Why would...? Because you're a pureblood, and it matters little if you're sometimes a human or not, right?"

"Yes, if anyone touches you during that time, excluding my family, they'd be dead. Especially if anyone meant you harm. We're very protective of our mates, and any female too." She looked around the room, and he could almost hear her mind working out the details of what he'd just told her. "Emma, you should know that I can't lie to you or harm you. I mean, it does happen that mates hurt each other, even kill, but we won't. Not ever, under any circumstances."

"I've heard that. And I think I know that you'd never hurt me, I mean you won't, but I don't think you would even if it wasn't in your blood." He nodded. "Liam, when we have a baby, if we have one, what happens? I mean, your brother was freaked out. Is that him or just in general?"

"Him. Mac has been a worrier since we were kids. Now if it were Riordan acting that way, I'd be concerned. I think that Storm would hit him if he was, but that's another story." She laughed, which was what he needed her to do. "We're all calm, for the most part, but this is the first for any of us. A child, grandchild, being born into this family. I think we're all a little stressed out."

"I'm sort of afraid, if you want to know the truth. Having a baby is scary work, I guess. I worry about having a little tiger in the house." He told her there were benefits to that as well.

"Like what? I mean, will this kid be as rambunctious as the rest of you?"

"More than likely. But I was talking about how you'd feel afterwards. You're a tiger and you'd heal very quickly. And you'll never get fat or overweight. Not that that's a bad thing, but because you burn a lot more energy, you will stay slim longer. And speaking of that, you'll live longer as well. Not forever, but longer." She was overwhelmed, he could see that, and when she lay her head on his shoulder, he just held her. It was going to be a long wait, he thought, and everyone was going to be tired by the end of this.

~~~

Mason would like nothing better than to rip the man's, Burt Hudson's throat out, but he'd promised Browning that he'd be good. To a point, he would, but for now he was just keeping an eye on the man for Emma. She had touched a place in his heart that even Browning hadn't been able to breach.

She was tender, yet one of the strongest women he knew. Even more so than Browning. He hated to keep comparing her to the other woman, but he knew so few that she was his only measuring stick. While Emma saw things from several windows, Browning saw one. Her distrust in people had saved her life and his a great many times over the years, but Emma would be just as lethal once she figured out her abilities. And those alone were enough to get her into hot water with many people, not to mention laboratories that would want to study her. And they would. Then when they had done all they could to the young tiger, she'd be as dead as the rest of the lab specimens that they had taken.

Burt moved to the barn when he'd figured out that he couldn't get into the house. He'd been at Liam's home for the past hour, and now he was finally making his move. Up until then he'd only been walking around the big house, staring in windows and making an ass of himself.

There were cameras all over the place. Burt had been recorded since he'd entered the property. The wolf pack that roamed the area was also on alert...to watch, not engage. Mason figured that was a good thing since he was sure that Burt's death would solve nothing, but his trial and jail sentence would close a lot of things. Especially for young Emma.

He heard him cursing and pulled shadows around him to see what he was up to. As soon as he entered the barn where not only Burt was but Emma's rig also, he nearly laughed out loud. The handful of keys the man had on him were not going to work any longer. As he watched, Mason wondered what sort of person would think that after you burned them once, they'd let you do it again.

"Dadburn kid. What in the world did she go and change the locks for? Didn't she want her old man to make a living?"

More than likely Emma did, but not at her expense. As the man continued to berate his child for taking care of herself and not him, he reached out to Liam to let him know what was happening.

It almost makes me want you to let him in the rig so we can get him on grand theft too. The man is a moron. And I can't believe that Emma is related to that man. She's so much different than him that it's laughable. Mason said he thought he was much too stupid to be only a moron. *He's also self-serving and clueless.*

He is at that. Currently, he is using every key on his impressive ring to try and unlock the door, while wondering aloud why Emma would do such a thing. Does he even realize that she'd have a reason to keep him out? And make it so that she's not in trouble again for his actions? Liam said more than likely not. *Men like him are the reason that I avoid humans at all costs. When do you think this thing with him will be finished where he is in jail for his crimes?*

The Whites are gathering a list of things that were on the shipments that were never received. Also, there is a list of complaints on the things that were delivered as well. Such as used and broken merchandise. Some of it not even what he left with. Most of those are companies that just want to be paid for what happened. I'm hoping when all this comes out, the businesses will be able to make things right with their insurance companies. Right now, it looks as if they have sent out bad items. With him being taken to task, the insurance company will have someone else to go after. I know that Whites will. They're who the family is working with. Mason asked him about the other things he had in his fire. *There are four buildings that I looked into for you in the area. One of them is occupied by a few homeless, but nothing that we can't handle. The others are empty, but one of them is hardly worth the money to purchase. I can see if I can get them to throw it in with the others at no cost, but I wouldn't buy it.*

Good deal. He watched Burt for a bit longer. *How are the new parents coming along? A child yet?*

No, Ennis has gone back several times, but nothing so far. She's progressing is all we know for sure. Mason told him to keep him informed. *I promise I will. You keep safe, Mason. I don't want him to get into the house, but I don't want you hurt either. You're a good friend.*

As are you, Liam.

When the connection was closed, he continued to watch the man. Now he was climbing over the rig, trying to see inside of it. If he were to fall, on his own, he wondered if he'd break his fool head or the concrete beneath him. Smiling, he figured the latter of the two would more than likely occur.

When he made his way back to the house, Mason stayed where he was. If he was stupid enough to break into the home, he'd never get out again. The police had been informed of what was going on, and were at this moment monitoring the cameras. For now, Mason figured that it was a waiting game, and when it was over, Burt would go to prison. That would be settled, along with what he had Liam working on. Mason thought of the work that Liam had been doing for him over the last several weeks.

Since he'd met the man, he'd been intrigued by his ability to make money. He didn't just turn a penny into a buck, but took the same penny and made millions off it. And he had a reputation that went with his good luck, as he called it. Mason thought it was much more. Liam wasn't just good, but scary good at what he did.

Not that he needed the money, but Liam had turned his into double what he'd had before. It was fun, really, to see him at work, how he researched every detail and made notes on notebooks of paper before making a move. The few times he'd talked to him about something, Liam had been prepared to answer any and all questions he might have, and a good accounting of information. Like the buildings in the area he was looking to purchase.

Mason would have simply bought them all, torn down what he didn't want, and moved on with his projects. He would have overpaid, he knew now, which wasn't really a terrible thing, but Liam had guided him into making a sound decision. And Mason had no doubt that it would be.

He was going to use the buildings for some ideas that he'd been thinking on for a bit now. One of them would be to get rid of some of the things that he'd collected over the years. Not all of them were antiques, but a great many of them were. Also, he had jewelry and other items, such as cars and such, which he no longer had any need for. Then the money could go for things that the Harrisons would think useful for their little town.

A school fund had recently been set up, as well as a new library fund. This was one of his favorite charities. Mason loved to read more than he did anything else. There weren't even televisions in his homes. Just stacks and stacks of books, along with lines of shelves for them. And Mason had a great many first editions that he might be willing to part with for the right amount of money.

By now Burt was on the porch again. He was scratching his head like he was confused as to why no one was answering the door. Mason wanted to tell him that he needed to think, but he was kind of afraid that Burt might explode or something. The man was incredibly stupid. When he made his way to the wooded area again, Mason had started to follow him when the man stopped.

There was something he was looking at. Mason wasn't sure what it could be unless one of the wolves had gotten too close, so he stepped out of the barn and looked as well. Some of the pack were there, but he doubted very much that Burt could see them. Then there was a small movement.

The woman was thin, much too thin for her height. As he watched her, he kept an eye on Burt as well. The man wasn't armed, he didn't think, but he wasn't going to count on that. When she stood up, Mason took a small step toward her when Burt yelled.

"What are you doing here?" She just stared at him. "You heard me. What you doing here? This here is my daughter's place, and she'll not like you coming around here without her being here."

She only stood there, staring at Burt like she knew him, which Mason was sure she didn't, because Burt didn't know her. Perhaps he had done something to her and she was seeking revenge. Mason moved so that he was behind Burt but still able to see the woman.

I'm not here for him. Mason nodded, shocked that she had spoken to him. *I've only been staying here to hide out. Nothing as terrible as it sounds, but I needed a break from life. I saw him and worried he was up to no good.*

He is, I'm afraid. She nodded but said nothing more. *Does any of the household know that you're here? I would hate for you to be caught by one of the pack and be harmed.*

They know me. He started to ask her what that meant, but she turned to her left and he did as well. Looking back to where the woman had been standing, he was surprised and amused that she was gone. She'd tricked him. *Vampire, you should know that the man you are watching, he means harm to the woman that lives there. I would watch him carefully, should I be you.*

I am forever careful. And this man only poses a threat to himself. The household, nay, the entire town knows he is just days away from getting his comeuppance. The woman laughed, and Mason felt his head spin just a little, like magic had danced over his skin and mind. *You are well?*

He got no answer, but found himself wanting to find her. No other reason would come to his mind, but he did have a powerful need to find her. Remembering his task, he turned to find Burt again. The man was nearly too easy to follow.

Burt left the area and he followed him. When he moved to the back of the hotel he'd been staying at, he knew that he was avoiding the owner. Randal, an old friend and the owner of the place, had told him several days ago when he'd gone to play chess, that the man was a deadbeat. Mason paid his bill, but asked that Burt not be aware of it as yet. Perhaps, he told the younger man, he'd fall going in out of the place and break his neck.

After seeing that Burt was settled in for now, Mason went to the pack. He wanted to know who the woman was. Needed to know that she was.... He wasn't going to lie to himself. Mason just wanted to know about her. To see if she needed anything, living in the woods like she was. It wasn't like him to care about someone that he'd never met. It bore looking into deeper.

Rick Danner had been pack master for only a few months. He was doing a good job of getting his wolves employment, educations, as well as good sturdy homes. As soon as Mason was let into the room Rick was in, he sat down across from him and handed him a box of cigars. The man loved the nasty things.

"You want something from me. And I know what it is." Mason nodded. "She contacted me about five minutes ago, telling me all about this vampire that was on the Harrison property. And the other man too."

"Can you tell me her name?" Rick said no. "I thought as much. You do know that I can get it from you, correct? And the fact that she knows I'm a vampire means that she would know that as well."

"I'd say that is all correct, but you can't get what I don't have." He didn't bother looking then. "She only needed a place to rest. I know nothing about her other than she's never caused us any trouble in the last few weeks that she's been here. We watch her...not over her, but keep an eye on her, nothing else. She doesn't interact with the other pack members, nor does she make a very big print when she stays in a spot."

"She cleans up after herself." Rick said it was more than that, she didn't do anything but add to her campsite. "You mean she's magical."

"Yes, I'd say that was about right. She might be something,

but I don't know what. Like I said, she leaves nothing of herself behind when she leaves an area. Even when she fishes, she cleans up the mess and feeds what is left over from her chore to the earth. We can find her, but we don't have a bead on where she might be at any given time." Mason asked him if he thought that was odd. "Odd? No, I wouldn't say odd, but I would say cautious. I think she's hiding from herself more than from someone."

"She looks to be too thin. Is she eating enough, you think?" Rick told him that he knew that she was smallish when she approached him. But if she was getting smaller, he didn't know. He'd not seen her since the first time. "I should like to speak with her. She knew what I was, and was able to converse with me through a link."

"She can me too. Letting me know when there is someone on the property that shouldn't be there. I was informed when both you and Hudson showed up, what he was doing, and then when he left. And like I said, she let me know you were there as well." Mason nodded. "I can tell you that she's been here about a month. When she was first here, I thought a husband or boyfriend was going to come around. But nothing yet. And for some reason, I don't think anyone will show up."

"Why not?" Rick just shrugged. "I really would like to speak to her. In person. If you could contact her, let her know that I'm asking about her, I'd appreciate it."

"I can do that, but I wouldn't expect her to come around. She's very private and stays to herself. If she wants to see you, however, it'll be on her terms, not yours." He asked if he knew what she was. "Nope. Woman, and a very pretty one at that, but I'm sure you've figured that out as well."

Mason sat there for several minutes, talking with Rick, but his mind was on the woman. She had spoken to him. That both bothered and intrigued him at the same time. There were only a few beings that he knew of that could do that. And he wanted to know —

"Mason?" He looked at Rick, realizing that he had zoned out of their conversation. "I told you that she said she'd meet you."

"Yes, yes, of course. When did she say?" Rick told him she'd contact him soon. "Thank you. I don't.... There is something about her that makes me need to see her."

Rick was laughing when he left. The man was under a great deal of stress, he supposed, to find his dilemma so funny. As he made his way back to his lair, he wondered not for the first time why he was still on this earth. There was nothing holding him but friendship. Mason supposed that was enough, but he wanted more.

CHAPTER 10

Liam looked through the nursery window and stared at the babies. He'd always thought of babies as being little tiny duplicates of their parents. Like someone had stuck them in the drier and they were shrunk down. They had all the parts of their parents, yet smaller and softer.

Liam looked at Ennis when he cleared his throat.

"You want one of these for your own?" He told him they had talked and were waiting. "No, I mean, one of these. The little boy with the blue tag without a name on it was left here. In a few days, someone from children's services will come for him and he'll be put in the system."

"Did they not want him? I mean, no one in their family?" Ennis said that when it happened, they didn't ask questions. "Will they be allowed to think it over and then return for him?"

"No, once they make the decision to abandon him, then they have to sign him over to us. Once that happens we take care of him for a period of time necessary before we call for someone to take him." Liam looked at the little boy while his brother continued. "He's healthy, if a little underweight. Eats well, and there are no drugs in his system."

"You check for that?" Ennis said they'd check on Andi's baby too. "I guess there is a lot of that going on now. If no one takes him, what happens to him?"

"He'll hit the system. More than likely he'll not be adopted out, at least I don't think so. Once he leaves here I have no say over anything, but I do get to check on him once a month for a year." Liam wanted to touch the little man. "So, I ask again, would you like him?"

"I'd have to ask Emma." Ennis said he'd hope so. "I never thought of adopting a child. I mean, I guess it only occurred to me to have a child with Emma."

"Most people don't think about adopting unless they can't have children for some reason or another. Most, but not all. You'd not believe how many babies we get in here that need to be in a home other than the one that they're born to, yet there is little to nothing we can do about it." Liam nodded. "Would you like to hold him?"

"I'd better not." Ennis asked him why. "Because you know as well as I do that if I do, he's as good as mine."

"Yeah, that's the point." He looked at his brother. "His parents were tigers, but not full blooded. I noticed that you didn't ask, but that's what he is. The family, none that are from around here, weren't purebloods, like I said, and at this point I have no idea what, if any, tiger is in him. He's not going to be able to go to a human household without them knowing what he is. I think that, more than anything, will keep him from joining a family."

"You are playing unfairly." Ennis laughed. "I'll talk to Emma. Do you know how much longer Andi and Mac are going to be?"

"Anytime now."

Ennis walked away and he stayed watching the baby. The other babies were fussing. Two of them were crying, and he just lay there. When he was joined by Emma at the window, he was sure that Ennis had sent her.

"No, he didn't say anything other than to tell me where you were when I asked." He nodded. "What are you doing here? Are you thinking of kidnapping one of these for us? I want a little boy, if you get to pick."

He told her what Ennis had told him. "Ennis seems to think that him being a tiger, no matter how much of one he might be, he'll not be adopted. They'd have to know, just in case he was one, to know how to deal with it."

"He wants us to take him?" He told her that was what he said. "And even though we know nothing about children, he thinks we'd be good at it? I don't. I mean, I might be a good mom, but I have no idea. What about you?"

"I don't think I'd make a good mom either. I don't have all the necessary parts, first of all. Then there is the fact that I have whiskers." She slapped him. "He asked me if we wanted to hold him. Do you?"

She nodded, then shook her head. Then nodded again. Before she could change her mind again, he knocked on the window and pointed to the little boy. The nurse nodded and came to get them. Once they were in a room, just the two of them, he thought of all the things that might go wrong with this. The nurse entered pushing a little cart in front of her almost as soon as he decided to run. Far and fast.

"We've been calling him Edward. At the first of the year we pick out twenty-six names, each with the next letter of the alphabet, to name such children." The little bundle in the bassinet didn't stir when the nurse pulled the blanket off him. "He's a good little boy. Never cries unless he's hungry. Or wet. Here you go."

The nurse handed Edward to Emma first. And when he

opened his eyes and looked up at her, Liam fell in love. Christ, he was beautiful. The nurse was still talking, but he wasn't listening. Liam couldn't take his eyes off the little boy in his wife's arms.

"Oh, Liam, he's so handsome, don't you think?" He did, and touched his fingers to his soft looking cheek. Pulling the little bonnet off his head, he laughed when he saw all the hair he had. "Look, he has the same hair color as you do."

The baby stared at them both, his little eyes going back and forth between them as they spoke softly to him or about him. Liam wanted to take him right now, go home, and hold him until he was too big to hold. When Emma handed Edward to him, he leaned back in the rocker and touched his fingers. His hand wrapped around Liam's finger like he was holding on in case they left without him. Liam knew as surely as he was sitting there that he had a son.

"He'll need a bottle soon." Liam nodded, reaching blindly for the bottle when it was handed to him. "He doesn't take much. We're a little worried about that, but we all think it's because he thinks no one wants him. Poor little tyke."

The baby latched onto the nipple like he was starving. As he drank the two-ounce bottle down, he never stopped staring at him. And when he closed his eyes finally, Liam looked over at Emma, who was crying.

"I want to take him home." She nodded and touched Edward's face. "We need him as much as he's going to need us."

"Yes, I have already fallen in love with him. Can we really take him?" The nurse, who had never left them, said that they could tomorrow, after the paperwork was done. "Yes, do what you need to do for us to take him home."

"We don't normally do this this way, just so you know. But we all know you and know that you'll be good to him." She fussed around with the bed. "Ennis told us that he'd never make it to the system, that one of his family would take him. He said that you were all tight, and that you'd never abandon a little one in need."

They held him until the nurse said he needed to be changed and weighed. Emma put him in the little crib and they sat there for several minutes, neither of them saying anything. They had a lot to do, he realized, and was excited about it. When they left the nursery, Emma asked if they should wait on the announcement until after the baby was born.

"Yes, that's a good idea. We don't want to take away from Andi and Mac." He nodded. "But that doesn't mean that we can't get some work done too. I mean, we're going to be parents tomorrow, and we don't have anything to take care of him with."

"That's right. Nothing." She stopped walking and looked up at him. "We don't even have the right kind of car for a car seat, or even a single diaper to use. Nothing for him to wear to take him home in. Liam, we're going to have to do some serious shopping if we're taking him to our house tomorrow."

He was making notes on his phone as they entered the waiting room. Ennis was there, and when he nodded at him and told him they were going to do it, he hugged him. No one thought it was odd, and if they did, they didn't say anything. Mac came crashing into the room just as he and Emma were sitting back down.

"We're parents." Everyone cheered for him, and he was hugged by them all. His mom and dad asked about the baby and Andi, but all he said was everyone was doing fine. "Andi wants to see your faces when you see the baby. She said that she will tell you the name too."

"All right. How long do we have to wait?" Mac said they were getting her moved now. Dad asked if they could at least see their grandchild. "I mean, it is our first one."

"Just wait, Dad. Andi wants to show the baby off." Dad nodded, but he looked none too happy about it. Mac left them again and said that the nurse would come for them soon. Everyone was so excited that they didn't sit back down but mingled now, so excited for the newest member of the family.

Twenty minutes later, a nurse in scrubs came to get them. She said that there was generally a rule about how many people could be in the room at once, but for this first time, they were making an exception. She led them to a room at the end of the hall, and they went in to see Andi laying with a bundle on her side, and not one speck of colored hat showing so they could know what the sex of the baby was. Not usually one to be so pushy, Mom went to the bed and pulled back the blanket.

"Well, my goodness, this is just unfair. You've kept us in the dark long enough, young lady." Andi laughed. "I don't think this is the least bit nice of you."

~~~

"Mom, Dad, I'd like to introduce you to my son, Cormac Andrew Harrison." Ordan looked at the little man and smiled. "He weighed six pounds three ounces."

"My goodness, son, such a tiny little thing. But he'll fatten up soon enough. We have to go fishing, him and me." Ordan was handed the baby and he felt his heart just take a tumble. "My oh my, what a beautiful little guy you are."

"Mom?" Ordan glanced at his wife and started to hand the baby to her when she was sobbing. Women did go on sometimes. But he looked at his son when he handed her a bundle too, this one in all pink. "Mom, this is Elizabeth Briana Harrison. She outweighed her brother by one ounce, coming in at six pounds four ounces."

"Twins? You had.... Oh Mac, you guys have twins?" Ordan

felt his love just about spill out his eyes. Crying wasn't an emotion that he had often, but for this he pulled out his hanky and rubbed his eyes hard. "My land, two little grandchildren, and here I am with only a fishing pole for one of them."

Ennis cleared his throat and Ordan looked at his son. "There is more news too, Mom and Dad. Liam? Why don't you tell them what you and Emma have done?"

"Tell us what? You're not breeding, are you, honey?" Emma shook her head and her face turned a fine shade of pink. "I'm sorry, child. I'm not usually so.... Why don't you tell us your news? I'd surely like to hear it."

When she stepped out, he thought for sure that he'd insulted her. He was ready to hand the baby back to Andi and go tell her he was surely sorry when she came back, holding her own little bundle, another blue one. She handed him to Liam and Ordan looked over his shoulder at the bundle in his son's arms.

"This is Edward Harrison. We haven't picked out a middle name yet, but we'll think on it. We get to take him home tomorrow." Ordan thought it was a joke and asked what was going on. Liam explained what had happened while he got to know his other grandson after he was handed to him.

"Three children at one time? My goodness, Ordan, we're going to have to get ourselves busy now. Think of all the fun.... Oh my, Christmas. Christmas will be so wonderful this year." He held his wife while she sobbed on his shoulder. Ordan looked around the room and smiled. There was nothing on this good earth better than having children and grandchildren, he thought.

The babies were fussed over. He thought he'd done a good job of not hogging them all the time, but he did have to hold them more than the rest. He was their granddaddy, wasn't he? And when little Emma brought him Edward, he just could not believe the luck he was having today.

"You okay with this?" He asked her what she meant. "He's not your biological grandchild. I mean, I know you have the other two, and we'll have one soon too, but I wanted to make sure you would be all right with him calling you Grandda."

"I wouldn't expect him to call me.... Are you asking me on account'a your own daddy? Because I have to tell you, darling, I'm as happy as I can be right now, and don't see a lick of difference between this one and the other two over there. They're my grandbabies, and I dare one person to try and tell me different." Emma smiled at him. "You were worried I'd not treat him the same?"

"No, not worried. Scared I guess, that.... Not you, Ordan, never you and Bri, but my dad is gonna have a lot to say when he finds out." He nodded, waiting for her to get to the point of her story. "He'll try and harm him. I know that now. He'll hate that he's going to be taking up my time that he thinks I should be spending with him."

"Your aunt talked to you." She nodded and played with the baby's cheek instead of looking at him. "Emma, there is nothing in this world that I'd do to any of my grandkids, nothing that would have anyone thinking that I favored one over the other. And so long as we can sit with them some, I don't care if he's blue or orange, he's my grandson."

She kissed him on the cheek and he held her and the baby. Someday he hoped that he got to have a conversation with her daddy. He'd show him the real meaning of loving. To think that a man like him had had anything to do with such a sweetheart just boggled the head bone.

When she left, leaving him with Edward, Eunice sat down beside him. Handing over the little man, he watched her cuddle him and touch him. When Edward sighed heavily and rolled his little head onto her plump bosom, she looked at him.

"I've never held a baby before." He told Eunice she was doing a right fine job of it. "They want me to live with them. I wasn't sure I wanted to, but now, with this guy there, I think I might do it. They could use an extra hand at times, I'm thinking."

"Yes, I just bet they could. So long as you share with us. You know, they already think of you as aunt to the other two as well. Got you a whole passel of babies to cuddle with."

Eunice nodded and Ordan told her she was going to be fine. "I don't know what to do about Burt. He's going to hurt them all now."

"He won't get within a foot of them. You either." She nodded and looked at Edward. "And if he thinks of touching that baby, I'll kill him. Not a threat there, but a promise. I will tear him apart and not feel the least bit sorry for it. Nobody, but nobody, hurts what is mine."

"He'll go on like it wasn't what he wanted to happen. That it was an accident." Ordan knew that. He'd heard the story from his son. "And when he is done, he'll walk away without a thought to how he'd hurt anyone. Like what he did to his own daughter."

"He'll get what's coming to him. See if he doesn't." Ordan wanted to tell her what he knew, how they were working with the police and the federal men to get him caught up with his pants down, so to speak. But she was hurting enough, and this was her big brother no matter what he'd done. "You just let the professionals handle it. Stormy and Nikki, they know what they're about."

The nurses came in a bit later and gathered up the babies. They needed to get some work done on them, and he wanted to go shopping. As they were headed out the door, Riordan stopped him. And when he took him to an empty room, he knew something had happened.

"Nothing bad." He nodded. "I promise, Dad, it's nothing bad. But Liam and Emma are going shopping to get things for their son, and I thought we could pitch in and help out."

"What did you have in mind?" He told him about their car, as well as some of the things that he'd helped Mac purchase and set up. "You thinking they might need some screwdrivers and such?"

"Yes, it took Mac nearly three hours to put the bed together at his house. And he's going home tonight to put the second one together before he brings his children home. Then there is Liam and all the things he needs done too." Ordan said they'd make an evening of it. "I had hoped that you'd say that. I was going to go look at cars with Liam, and if you could get the rest of them gathered up to work at first Mac's house, then we'll move on over to Liam's. I think his will take the most work."

"I'm on it. And you should tell them girls to take Emma out shopping too. She's gonna need diapers and sleepers. Good heavens, boy, they're going to need everything by the morning." Riordan nodded. "We'll get them set up. You see to the car and let me organize the rest."

"Thanks, Dad. And congrats on being a grandda. Three times."

He was still smiling as he made his way to his car. He was going to be the best grandda he could be.

By midnight they were gathered in what was going to be Edward's room. Boxes were everywhere, and they just looked to him like they were going to be days getting these things together. There was a rocking chair just sitting all by its lonesome. A dresser that was covered in some kind of plastic stuff, and a mattress.

"Well now, we got to get the bed put together, don't you think?" Ordan set Darcy and Ennis on that. "You two get started on that other thing. What is that, anyway?"

"Chest of drawers, when it's together." He glanced over at the dresser that was in the corner and asked why a baby would need two of them. Liam laughed. "Did you see what Mom bought today? We'll be lucky if we don't have to buy a third one. And that is a shelf for things like toys, and to hold things like diapers and wipes. We have a lot of those too."

He started on the shelf. It was blue, and he was amazed at the ease with which it went together. There were decorations for the wall that Emma was putting up, and Stormy was putting together a diaper bag from a list on her phone. Ordan thought this might be good for all of them, getting a taste of how they worked together.

By sunrise the room was ready. The car seat had been strapped inside the new car, the bags packed up for the babies to come home with, and there was even a big stuffed tiger for each of them in their rooms that his wife had gotten them, with big ribbons on them with their names. He knew she'd be doing something special, and was glad that she'd found them all tigers.

Ordan sat in the rocker and looked around Edward's room after his kids left to take a nap. He wasn't surprised to see Liam come in and sit in the other chair in the room with him.

"Thanks, Dad." He told him it was nothing. "I don't mean for just tonight. I mean for every day of my life. For being there for me when I was a kid. As an adult, you never told me what I wanted to do with my life was wrong. You were and always will be my hero. And I can only hope that my son and the rest of my children feel half as much love for me as I do for you."

Ordan looked at the big stickers on the wall. Lions, tigers, bears, and other animals were smiling and colorful. He needed a moment, his heart and throat were all clogged up with emotion right then.

"You remember that teacher you had? Mr. Walnut, I think that was his name." Liam told him. "Yes, that's it, Pecan. I knew he was a nut of some sort. Do you remember him telling me that you weren't going to amount to a hill of beans with your head in the clouds like you were all the time?"

"Yes, he seemed to think that me trying to figure out an easier and faster way to do things wasn't right. That if I just followed the instructions and rules, I'd be able to make my way in the world or it would crush me." Ordan nodded and pulled one of the stuffed animals off the shelf and held it in his hands. "Dad, I will never forget what you told him."

"Me either, the old fool." They both laughed. "Telling him that your head in the clouds was going to be the next best thing to sliced bread. That you thinking on your own was better than anything I could have hoped for. And you know what I did when you made your first million? I went back there and I told him about it. Told him that he wasn't fit to be a teacher if he was going to stagnate his students."

"You really came through for me that day. And every day since then. In big ways and small ones, forever." Ordan nodded and rocked in the rocker. "I'm going to be a good dad to my kids, and only because you were the best dad for me."

"You're going to make this old man cry like a little one if you keep that up." Liam stood up and hugged him tightly. "I love you, son. As much as I tell you that, I sometimes don't feel as if I say it enough. I love you all, so very much, and consider myself the luckiest man in the world to have had you all call me Dad."

"You'll have to think on what the grandkids will call you

too." He asked him what he meant. "Well, you have three right now. Do you wanna be Grandpa? Grandda? Pops? Whatever you want, that's what they'll call you."

"I can have them.... Well, I got me a few weeks here. I'll give it some serious thought. Right now, I'm leaning towards Pops, but you never know. I might go back and forth until something sets with me." Liam was still laughing when he left him there. Ordan thought of all the trouble him and these three were going to get into.

He might have to get on the others to get them going too. No sense in just having three of them. Ordan thought he would wait a bit…not long, but a little bit. Nikki was breeding, he knew that. And if he didn't miss his bet, Stormy would be soon, too.

"Now there will be a hellion when it's born. Won't even matter if it's a girl or boy, they'll be just like their momma." Ordan rocked a little harder, thinking of the fun he was going to have now. "Yes, siree, I'm going to be in so much trouble all the time when they get going with me."

CHAPTER 11

Willa watched the vampire. He wasn't being quiet, and she had a feeling that he was trying to make sure she heard him rather than him being clumsy in the woods. He stopped after a few seconds and she looked in the same direction he was, and knew that he'd seen her tent. Flying down to the ground, she stood ten feet from him as she shifted.

"I wasn't sure where you were going to meet me. The woods aren't the first place I would have asked to see you." Willa said nothing and sat on the ground. Mason did as well, unheeding of his suit or the cost of it. "Rick said that you knew my name, but he didn't know yours."

"Willa. Like you, I don't have a last name that I can remember." He nodded and she looked at him. "I've been taking a rest here. Life has gotten to be too much for me. I needed this."

"I'm sorry. I feel that way a great deal as well. I usually just go to sleep." She nodded and asked him if he was happy with the new ones, the babies. "Yes, they're beautiful. You should go and see them. I'm sure that they'd welcome you."

"They would." She wasn't sure how to bring up the next subject, so she did it like she did most things, bluntly. "I'm your mate."

"Yes, I know. It took me a while to figure it out, I'm ashamed to say." Willa let her breath out that she'd been holding...he believed her. "Once I had, I had to think about what that would mean for us. You aren't human and neither am I. You're also not vampire, if I don't miss my bet."

"Nay, not vampire. I'm all things." He nodded. "I think I am what is called an elite shifter. I can be a vampire should I wish it, but I don't care for it for myself. It.... I don't feed well on just blood."

"Neither do I anymore. I can eat foods when I choose, but I don't. It's.... I don't think it's because the food isn't good, but I don't like the full feeling that I get from it." Willa said she felt the same. "What do you eat?"

"Mostly greens, but I can eat meat. Again, I don't eat much for the same reason that you don't. It fills me up too much." He said that he understood. "What do we do now, Mason?"

"Honestly? I don't know. I should feel something for you. Not that I don't want you, but I don't know what it is just yet. Protective. Scared. Not of you, but of the unknown. I'm a very old and powerful vampire that has seen much in my years." She told him she was old too. "Yes, I figured that out as well. Are you happy? About finding me?"

"I'm not sure about that either. You aren't what I expected. I don't know what it might have been, but you weren't it." He told her he knew the feeling. "I had given up on ever finding my other half."

"As had I. If not for the Harrison ambush, I think I would have, long ago, ended my time here. Browning, she is the wife of the leap leader, she was my only friend for a great many years." She asked about his home. "I have numerous ones that I use, but I own some as well. There are several that I use when going home is not an option, or if I'm too exhausted."

Willa stood up when he did, asking if he'd like to take a walk with her. She laughed when he asked if they could not walk in the woods where there were so many eyes. She asked if he wanted to go to his home. When he put out his hand, she didn't hesitate in taking it into her own much smaller one. The tingle startled her a bit, but he just smiled at her and they made their way out of the wooded area.

"I would like that, I think. I can show you around, and if you aren't satisfied with it, I can find something more suitable for the two of us." She nodded, thinking it very strange that he would do such a thing for her. Not that it mattered, she supposed. "I don't know a great deal about what it is like to have a mate. My own parents were not the best of role models."

"I have been alone much longer than I have been with people, so I find that I am ignorant of how to interact with them as well. Even you might be frustrated with me should you wish to have a conversation. I don't speak much." He said that he was the same, only talking when necessary. "We are more suited than I thought we'd be."

"Yes, we are." They talked about nothing much of anything. Mostly of what they had done to be here in this time. And of the Harrisons. "You will enjoy their company for a little bit. They are loud, overbearing at times, but they love with all their hearts. I find them to be fun just to watch from a distance. They are having an issue at the moment with the father of the newest mate. He is not to be trusted."

"The man you were with the other day." He nodded, telling her his name. "I have seen him about. He is sneaking around the household more boldly daily. I nearly fell upon him last night when he was sitting on the ground watching the goings on of the house. He has not guessed there will be a baby there soon."

"Emma, the mother, thinks he will harm it in an effort to make her his again. Not sexually, but he is selfish about the time that he gets to spend with her. But the police are after him as well. They're gathering up the things they need before they arrest him." Willa asked him why that would matter. "It will be closure for a great many things that he has done. He has stolen from a lot of businesses. Also, I think that Emma will feel better with him in prison rather than dead. He is her father, after all."

"Yes, I can understand that a little. But if he harms any of them, it will matter little to her then. Now that we are mates, I will, no doubt, be expected to protect them as well." Mason thanked her. "There is no need for thanks. Rick, the pack leader, said that they owe much to the ambush. That had it not been for them over the years, they might have had to move away. When humans don't understand something they try and kill it. Much like a lot of nonhumans."

They were nearly to the town, and she looked around for cameras and such. Not that she thought it would harm her, but she didn't care to have her image taken. As they made their way to the lower levels of a grand yet old house, he stopped talking. She was nearly too busy to notice until they were shut up in his rooms.

Willa kissed him. He was very good at it, and she found herself wanting more of the man, of his body as well. Pulling back, she looked at him and wondered why she had agreed to this. He was nothing like she had been told.

"I want you." Nodding, she moved to his bed. "Can you strip for me? I'd love to watch you."

He was calm in his demands. She wasn't sure what to think of that either. As she began to take off her shirt, she smiled at him. Soon this would be done, and she could move on with her life.

The bed was huge, much larger than any she'd ever seen. Asking him about it, he told her that he was a big man and needed the room. As he stripped himself, she noticed scars on his body, deep and long, and reached out to touch one of them.

"The disadvantages of being very old. When I was younger, I would use my magic to heal such things. Now I see no reason to bother with them. They are, after all, just history for me." She ran her finger over the one that seemed to have only missed his heart by a hair's breadth. "Someone long ago decided that he wished me dead."

When he laid back on the bed, she slid her body over his. She wanted to be on top, her body joined with his. As she licked his cock, thick and hard, he moaned and rocked his hips up to her mouth. Taking him into her, she sucked hard on him while fondling his heavy sac. This was going to be wonderful, she knew it.

"Please, ride me." Willa smiled. As she moved up his body, she used her magic. Soon, she told herself, soon they would be joined. "Please?"

Her body fit over his, and he filled her in ways she'd never felt before. The magic in the room was thick, but he was too enthralled with her to notice. As the slim stake filled her hands, she rode him harder, faster until she was nearly lost in the moment. Bringing the stake down to his chest, she closed her eyes.

"My father will meet you in hell." He cried out, and she knew he was moments from his own death. And when his hand curled around her throat, his nails bit deeply into her. She was going to die, she knew it. But it would be worth it to know that this monster was dead as well.

~~~

Emma sat up in the bed. She wasn't sure if she was going to scream or if she already had. Looking over at Liam when he sat up, she remembered the baby. Jumping out of the bed, she ran to his crib only to find him sleeping soundly, his little body safe.

"What was that?" She said she didn't know. Then she thought of Mason. "Mason, something happened to Mason."

Agreeing with Liam, she grabbed her robe and made her way down the staircase. She needed to get to him. Right now. There was a buzzing in her head, like a million voices talking at once, and she realized it was the rest of the Harrisons. Walking into the living room to find her keys, she screamed when she saw Mason lying on the floor.

"Hello, dear." She went to him and told the others in her head to shut up, he was with her. There was laughter then and she told him he was bleeding. Once the voices started shouting again, she cut them out. "They are concerned about me."

"As well they should be. What have you done to yourself?" He laughed and a small trickle of blood came from his mouth. "Mason, you die and I will never forgive you. You mean the world to me and this family. And what will poor Edward Mason do without you there to guide him?"

"You named your child after me?" She nodded, telling him that she and Liam had talked about it last night. "Hello, Liam. I seem to have spouted a leak here and there."

"Mason, you old fool. What do you need?" Mason closed his eyes when Liam moved to be beside the two of them. "The family is on their way to help you. Just hold on."

"She claimed to be my mate. I thought so too until I touched her. I knew then." Liam asked him what he was talking about. "Willa. I found her in the woods here. Well, found isn't the right

150

word. She was stalking me."

"You have a stalker?" He nodded at Emma and looked at her. "I don't understand, but perhaps you can hold off explaining until we get you healed. You need food. Blood."

"I do, but I cannot take from you, my dear." She started to ask him why not when Liam shoved his wrist to his mouth. "Liam, you know that I need more than you can give me. I'm sorry, but I think I would die rather than harm you."

"You take some from all of us. That way, none of us are harmed. Take what you need to stop the flow of blood." Mason nodded and bit into Liam's wrist. Almost as soon as he licked the wounds closed, the front door was opened and the family, all of them, gathered in the living room.

They lined up to feed the man. Emma never left his side, holding his hand through the entire ordeal. By the time he had drunk from all the men, she could see that his color was returning and that his skin was no longer clammy. Emma let out a long slow breath. They'd saved him. All of them working as a family had saved Mason's life.

"You have questions. I do have answers, but right now I must rest. I am all right, and the woman who has done this to me has been dealt with." He asked if he could stay the night. "I have a bit of a mess at my place at the moment."

He was moved to the lower levels of the house, Liam carrying him for the most part because he was simply too weak to walk. There was a nice suite down there, she'd only just started setting it up. Emma figured that when the family was gathered together, someone might want to sleep there.

As soon as Mason was on the bed, he took her hand in his. "You're going to have a baby." She shook her head. "Even the tiger does not have the abilities that I have. You are with child."

"I can't be. I mean, I know that we've had...I didn't go into heat." She felt stupid saying that, but Mason seemed to understand and kissed the back of her hand. "Are you sure?"

"As positive as I am about my friendship for you and your family." Emma put her hand over her belly and smiled. "You will need to take a care, my child. For the man who comes for you, your sire, he will not care a bit that you're carrying his next grandchild. Nor that you are happy."

"I am happy, and after talking with the family, I realize that my father isn't the man I thought he was. I mean, I knew that he was a selfish prick, but not to what extent. He means to have his way no matter what everyone around him has to give up in order for him to be happy and satisfied." He nodded and lay back on the bed. "Are you really all right, Mason? I would really hate for anything to happen to you."

"I am well. Smarter for today's events, but well. When night falls again, I will be rested and healed. I will then tell you the story." She nodded and kissed him on the cheek as she stood up. "Take care, Emma. I'm too weak to help you until I rise."

"Is he coming?" He said he thought he was already here. "I'll be careful. And he won't hurt me either. I know better than to trust him."

Emma made her way to the upper level and sat on the couch. Breakfast was being made, she could smell the bacon cooking in the kitchen. The family was all there with the exception of Andi, who was still resting at home. Her own son was in the arms of his dad and having his early breakfast.

"Mason needs to rest, he told me, and that he'd explain when he wakes tonight." She looked around when no one said anything. "You already know, don't you?"

"Rick told us about this woman that had wanted to meet

Mason. He went by Mason's home and...it looks like there was a fight and she tried to kill him. He...Mason killed her first. Rick said he feels responsible for it. He, I guess, told Mason she wanted to meet him. He and the pack are taking care of the mess." She nodded and asked what happened. Liam handed her the baby as he continued. "We don't know the details, not yet, but Rick said that he thought that Mason assumed that the woman was his mate. He said that he had too. He knows now that it was magic. But nothing more than that. She used magic to make herself look as if she was his mate to murder him. But as for the why, we'll have to wait."

"He told me to be careful, that my dad was here." Storm said that he was, and had been for a few days. "Figures. It would have been so easy for him to come up to the house and ask to see me, but he must do things the hard way. So he can look like the martyr, I think."

"He's been to the house, according to the cameras. He's not tried to break in, but it's only a matter of time before he tries. And I think us being here all the time lately is keeping him away. When he comes here, he'll want only you here to talk to you. His encounter with Liam and Dad the other day made him realize how big they are, and that they're not ones to mess with."

Emma went to the window and looked out. She wasn't sure she could see her dad out there, it was still a little dark, but his image popped out at her and she told Storm. Storm came up behind her and looked with her. She asked if there were wolves near him. They were red hot, like they looked when she was her tiger. It was the strangest thing, seeing them, as she was human now. It was just one more thing to add to her crazy shit list.

"Two that I can see. And he's armed. I don't know where he got it...I've never known him to carry a gun. But then, this freaky ability is new to me. He could have been all along." Storm said she was sorry. "I am too. I don't mean to snap at you. This isn't your fault."

"No, but I can't imagine how hard this is on you." She watched her dad, out there in the dark, stalking her. "He won't hurt you, Emma. None of you."

"I know that. I mean, I want to believe that he'd never hurt me, but I know now that he is capable of it. You just don't want to think of your own father trying to hurt you. I don't think he'll kill me. I have no idea, but I do think that but he will hurt Edward and Liam if he can." Storm said that was a sure bet. Emma looked at the baby in her arms. "I can't wrap my head around the fact that I have a son."

"Riordan and I are going to have one when I go into heat the next time." Emma congratulated her. "Not so fast. I'm still waiting to see how much trouble one of them is with you guys. I might chicken out. I've been in charge of men for too long to know what the hell to do with an infant."

"Yeah, I can see that. You can't just order them to sleep and expect them to do it." Storm asked her why not, and then smiled. "You're going to be a great mom. And when you get the chance, I'd like to learn how to shoot a gun. I'm not going to go into a fight next time with just my cat. That shit is getting old."

"Good for you. We'll do it in a couple of days when this is done with your dad." She asked if it was going to be done that soon. "Today, if I can manage it. The wolves are going to clean up at Mason's, then come back here to help him off the property. I think after that, he'll come to you. Places he's been staying aren't going to be as accepting of him once I'm finished."

"Thank you." Storm told her it was no problem. "I mean for being my friend. I don't have a lot of those in my life."

"You do now." She looked into the living room then back at Storm. "There isn't a person in there that wouldn't lay down their life for you, or anyone in your little family. I don't think it'll come to that, but your dad, he's not going to be able to take advantage of you again. Nor your aunt."

"Aunt Eunice is going to go on another trip soon. Not so far away, but she said she has some shopping to do now that she's a great aunt. I think Bri is going with her." Storm groaned and Emma laughed. "I want to hang out here and get to know my son. You should stay and protect me."

"Thank you." They were both laughing when they entered the living room again. Edward was asleep, and she put him in the crib that had been bought for this level of the house and entered the dining room. It was going to be a long day, Emma thought, but she was glad to have everyone here to start it off.

Emma had a lot of things to do today. Most of it was indoors, but she did go out in the back yard a couple of times. Liam had gone into town to see to some of the paperwork for her dad's arrest, and she played with the baby. Mostly she just watched him sleep or fed him, but it was so much fun she found her list of things to do being ignored in favor of holding the baby.

"How can anyone not want you?" She looked up when someone laughed a little. She'd not known that Ordan was here. "You think that people are just too busy for a baby, or selfish?"

"Both. But they're not bad people." She said she hadn't meant to sound like she thought that. "No, I know you wouldn't. But there are folks who are just as terrified of raising a baby as some are to go into a dark room. Bad memories, abusive spouse. There are any number of reasons that someone might give up a child."

"Ennis said that the couple who gave us Edward were part tiger, and not in a place where they could raise him on their own.

I'm sorry that they can't, but I'm glad that we were able to help them." Ordan asked if they were going to keep in contact with the couple. "No, they didn't want that. When they gave him up, they wanted to move on and try not to think of him. I don't know that I could do that."

"Me either." She gave him the baby when he asked for him. "I just needed me a little hold. I've been over to Mac's house, but there is just too much going on over there for me to get some loving in. Too many people for me to get a proper talk to them."

Emma left him to the baby. Ordan was telling Edward about something to do with his dad, and that they were going fishing. She made her way to the kitchen to find the cook. She was starving again, and it wasn't even noon. Emma thought she knew where some cookies were.

Just as she entered the room, she knew something was wrong.

"Hello, Hudson. I was wondering where you been." Her dad was sitting at the kitchen table with a gun in front of him, and Marla, their new cook, was fixing him breakfast. "I been worried about you. I thought I'd come see you and we could work some things out. You and me."

Emma sat when she was told, but reached for her family. This was going to be it, and she wasn't going to be stupid enough to think she could do it on her own.

Chapter 12

Burt wasn't happy about the turn of events. He wasn't happy about a lot of things, but this girl in front of him was lippy and mean to him. He asked her again if he could move in with them.

"No. And for the fifth time, hell no. I told you before, I'm done with you. You've fucked up my life enough, and I wrote you off." He told her she couldn't do that, he was her dad. "Dads do not forge their children's names to loans, then skip town with not just the goods, but with my good name. What the fuck were you thinking?"

"Hudson, I don't care for you talking like that to me. You'll stop cursing. That's a trucker thing, and one thing you told me was you weren't going to be like that. You were going to be nice." She said she was nice. "How do you figure that? You've been terrible to me since you came in here. What a way to treat me."

"You are getting what you deserve. And I'll curse all I want. I'm a grown ass woman." Burt shook his head. "Eat, then get out of here. Or better yet, why don't you step in front of a fast-moving truck and get out of my life?"

"I don't know what's come over you, but I don't care for it." Burt did, however, love the food he was eating. "When this thing is settled with you and me, I'd very much like to eat like this all the time. You know you can't stay mad at me. You're a very forgiving soul, you are."

"I talked to Mom." Burt dropped his fork and stared at his daughter. "You lied to me. You told me that she left us when I was a baby because she didn't care for being a mom. That was a lie. You nearly drained her dry of her money, and then you wanted more. You should have given me to her. She would have done me better, and certainly wouldn't have robbed me of everything I worked hard to get."

"I done you just fine. Look at you. You have a nice home. A lot of money. Speaking of which, I might need you to lend me some money for the hotel I was staying in. He said that someone paid some of it, but not enough to keep me there. If you can fork over about a grand, then I can take care of a few other things as well." She told him no, but he didn't care, she'd give in. She always did. "I've been thinking too. That rig of yours isn't doing you a bit of good sitting out there. Why don't you let me use it for a few runs? That way I'll be out of your hair while you get things set up for me here with you and that husband of yours. He gonna be gone a lot? I'm hoping so. If you don't want me to live here, then someplace else. I'm easy, you know that."

"I'm selling my rig. To someone that has a license to drive it and the money to pay for it." He nodded, knowing that since he'd planted the seed in her head, she'd let him have it for a song. Not that he'd have to pay her back or anything. Hudson was flush. "What were you planning to do with it anyway? You don't have a license to drive it. Not to mention there isn't a place within a thousand miles that will let you leave the lot with their goods. You fucked that up when you stole from a few of them."

"I'll find work. I'm like you, I land on my feet." She didn't say anything, which was fine by him.

A man walked into the kitchen, and it took him a moment to realize this was the husband. He didn't like him, so he ignored him when he sat at the table with a plate of food. "Anyway, as I was saying, I have big ideas now that I've had me a long rest. You won't believe how much money can be had out there that no one has tapped into."

"Perhaps because not everyone is a thief like you." Burt picked up his glass and asked for a refill as the man spoke again. "What is it you think your plans are, Burt? I'm assuming that you think you'll get money from us. You won't, by the way. Emma and I have decided that we'd rather burn it than give you anything."

"No, not you. You're not going to be involved with any dealings I have with my daughter." Burt drank his juice down and sat the glass on the table and reached for the gun. Before he could touch it, he heard a baby crying. "What the heck is that noise?"

"My son." An elderly woman came in and handed the baby to the man. He cuddled it a little before turning it over to Hudson. She had a look in her eyes that he'd not seen before. Like she used to look at him. "This is Edward Harrison, our son. He's your grandson too, I guess."

"I don't want any grandchildren. Holy smokes, Hudson, what the heck have you gone and done? And there isn't any way that that kid is related to me. You just have someone take it away from here." Hudson held the kid closer to her and it quieted down. He started to ask her if she'd smothered it when she glared at him. "What do you have this kid for, Hudson? You know that it's gonna be hard for me and you if you got him."

"He's my son, and I don't know what you think you and I are going to do, but I assure you, it won't be anything willingly." He looked at the kid, then at his daughter again. She sure believed that it was her son. "What do you want? If it's money, then no. If it's the truck, again, no. If you think you're living here, then hell no. Whatever else you might want, I think you can assume the answer to that is going to be no too."

"You're awfully selfish, Hudson." She told him to call her Emma. "Emma might be what these folks call you, but not me. I've loved calling you Hudson since you were born. To me, you're Hudson."

"I'm not even a Hudson any more. So, you calling me that is just dumb. I'm Emma Harrison. This is my husband, Liam Harrison. My son—"

"You don't have a son, darn it. You just don't. Now, if you could get back to what we were talking about before he came in here, then I can get things taken care of today that have needed my attention for a bit now." She didn't even look at him. "Hudson, you're not being nice to me."

When Eunice walked into the room, he grinned. Here was someone he could control, and he picked up the gun. She just smacked him in the back of the head and told him to behave. He'd never been so mistreated by his family in all his life. Burt didn't know what was going on, but there wasn't any way it was going to continue.

"You know better than to hit your big brother, Eunice. I'm not going to take it any better than when we was kids." She told him she should have hit him more. "What's gotten into you all? You're acting all stuffy. Like I'm nothing to you. I'm your elder and your father. You'll remember that."

"I don't have to remember anything, Burt. You've been a horrible person all your life, and you haven't improved at all since you've grown up. I had hoped that having a family might make a difference to you, but all it's done is make you stupid... well, stupider." Burt wanted to hit her too, but she started talking again. "Have you seen your grandson? He's a beautiful little man."

He didn't want to be a grandda. He wanted to be a man that ruled his family. It had been his thinking that once these people were out of the way, he'd be living the big life. But with this kid around.... Well, Burt thought he'd have to give some serious thinking on how to handle it all.

"I have me a list. I wasn't going to tell you this just yet, but I have lined us up some work that'll have us traveling together. It'll be a few days before I can gather up some clothing and stuff, but you can spot me some cash today and I'll go into town and start getting ready. About a grand." When she didn't tell him no, Burt went on with his needs. "I'll need to borrow a car too. That way nobody has to cart me around while I do some much needed shopping. I think you should pack for about a week. What do you think?"

"No." He was getting mighty sick of hearing her say that to him. "When are you leaving my home?"

"I don't have any cash yet." She told him unless he came here with it, he wasn't going to have any when he left. "Hudson, honey, you're being unreasonable. Why is that? What did I do to you to deserve you talking to your old man this way?"

"Seriously? Well, let's start from the beginning, shall we? My mom, first of all. You treated her badly, nearly ruined her financially, and then you lied to me about it. When I was in school you told me that the teacher that you knocked up was a bald faced liar, and that you'd never do that. I found out just the other day that not only was it your son, but when she lost him, you sent her a card of congratulations. Then there was the truck."

He asked her if she was going to bring that up every time he needed money. "Yes, as a matter of fact, I am. You stole from me. My house, my car. Then you hid out so that I'd have to explain all by myself why my own father wasn't to be trusted as far as he could spit."

"That's all water under the bridge now." She said that it wasn't. "Sure, it is. You took care of it, just like I knew you would. And if I get into a jam again, I know that you're going to be there for me. Just like Eunice has been. It's what family does."

"No, I don't think so, Burt. I'm done with you too." Eunice smiled over her cup at him and he winked at her. "You used up all your good will from me when you killed my husband."

"It was an accident. Don't you remember the police telling you that?" She sipped her drink and just stared at him. "Besides, he wasn't good for you, Eunice. He was taking up all your time. And there wasn't any way that he was going to love you like I did. You're better off without him sucking you dry."

"So you killed him. Why? Didn't you want me to be happy?" Burt looked around the room and couldn't figure out why they were all pouncing on him. "I asked you a fucking question."

"He wasn't going to make you happy. He had to go. And when I saw the opportunity, like I always do, I took it. That's what makes me a good planner and a man that gets things done his way." He looked at Lima, or Liam, whatever his name was. "You get in my way and that'll happen to you too, you know. I always land on my feet, just like a cat."

"Do you?" The husband stood up then…Christ, he was a big man. And when he pulled his shirt over his head, Burt looked at his daughter. She was cooing at that damned kid again, and he wanted to tear it out of her arms. "Perhaps I'm much better at landing on my feet."

He was gone. The man was.... He was a cat. Jumping back from him when he came at him, Burt screamed for someone to kill it. But when he reached blindly for the gun he couldn't find it, and noticed that Eunice had it and it was pointed at him.

"Sit down, Burt." He told her he wouldn't. "You either sit or I'm going to shoot you. Or Liam here eats you alive."

Urine filled his shoe, and he hated what they were doing to him. He looked at his daughter and asked her please to help him out of this mess. She shook her head.

"You can't tell me no, Hudson, this is a matter of life or death. This man is going to kill me. Can't you see that now? He's no good for you, like I told you. It's all about me." She handed the baby to the cook and she left with him. "There you go. Now let him out or tell Eunice to kill it, and we'll be all right then."

"You're going to prison." He asked her why. "For one thing, you committed fraud when you signed my name to the bank loan. Using my house that you had no rights to was the second thing you did. And then you started taking loads from companies and selling them for a profit. Then there is the attempted murder of myself, as well as the murder of Aunt Eunice's husband."

"Those companies have insurance for that kind of thing. Why on earth would anyone care if it was a load here or there? They got it back, ten times over I'd bet. As for killing anyone off? Why do you say those things to me? Your own father." She said nothing. "Hudson, I'm not going to forgive you easily for this here thing you're doing. You tell that man to go away, and you and I will talk about how you're going to drop the charges against me. And then I'll think about bringing you in on a couple of deals I got going. You can sure afford the best now. You don't know how much I miss that truck I had. It had room like you'd not believe. I'll order us both one...we'll have some good money

163

after that."

"I'm not going anywhere with you, and you won't be going anywhere either. You're only going to prison." He said that he wasn't. "I'm sure you think that, but you are. And I'm going to be happy as a clam to know that's where you ended up."

The police came in the kitchen then, and he asked them if they were taking the tiger away. When he was shoved on the table with his arms behind his back, he looked at Eunice. She was grinning at him like she was enjoying this.

"Eunice, you don't want to see me in jail, do you? I mean, we're going to have to catch up, you and me. I can't do that from a jail cell. Tell these men that you'll take care of whatever they think I did." She said no. "I'm sick of people telling me that, darn it. I'm your brother, your big brother. I deserve better."

"We all do, Burt. All of us deserve better than you."

He was still trying to get help as they took him out of the house. Darn it, they weren't going to be happy until he lost his temper. He didn't like to lose it, but they were pushing him. The moment he was shoved into the back of the cruiser, he thought things might not go as planned. At least not today. Burt would have to revise his plans, but like he'd told them, he landed on his feet.

~~~

Liam found Emma on the back deck. His family had left about an hour ago, and he'd been looking for her since. Edward was down for his nap now that he'd been fed. Sitting on the swing while she sat in the chair, he asked her if she was all right.

"I'm not sure." He nodded. "My dad, he really did think that I'd be fine with the mess he made and left me to deal with. Not to mention, he thought that it was just fine to threaten you and the rest of the family because they were taking attention from him."

Liam stretched out his legs, giving himself a moment to think of a response. He was sure there was one there, but for the life of him, all he could think of was telling her that her dad was a narcissistic prick.

"Dad said to tell you that he loves you." She smiled then, and he thought of something else. "My family was in the other room cheering you on while the police were waiting for him to confess. It wasn't the one that they thought they'd get, but it was enough to take him in. As soon as he got to the jail, he tried to hit one of the officers up for the deal of a lifetime. He only had to let him go and get the rig we're storing for him."

"He's not going to believe I'm not going to help him out even when he's behind bars." Emma stood up and walked to him and sat on his lap. "I just want to be held. Then I want to go in and pull Edward to my chest and hold him."

"I've put him down for his nap, and Aunt Eunice is keeping an eye on him. I think she's pretty hurt from all this as well." Emma said she was. "When she takes her trip, she begged me to take pictures at least a dozen times a day and send them to her. Not just of Edward, but of you and I as well."

"I'd very much like for you to take me to the woods and have your way with me." He smiled at her. "If you tell me you're not in the mood, I can—"

He rocked upward into her and she smiled at him. "I am never not in the mood when you're around me. There is not a moment that goes by that I don't want to strip you down and take you against any hard surface that I—"

"Less talking and more doing." He stood up and set her on her feet. "What do you want me to do?"

"Run." He let his cat take him, not caring at all if he didn't have anything to wear out there. As soon as she disappeared into the woods, he spoke to his brother, Riordan. *I'm in the woods with Emma. Could you please tell the pack to back off a bit?*

Yes, I can do that. I wanted to tell you that there are four emails for you. Well, the Harrisons, but you in particular. They're from the companies that you helped by finding Burt. The claims on their insurance can go through now. He said that he'd had a lot of help. *Perhaps, but you did the ground work, and I thank you for it.*

No problem. He stalked Emma, knowing that she was getting good at hiding from him. *Riordan, how did we survive without mates before this? I mean, they're everything, aren't they?*

Yes, they are. And Storm would tell us that we wouldn't have been able to.

He was laughing when he closed the connection. He had a wife to find and make love to.

He searched for nearly ten minutes before he found her. It wasn't that he wasn't trying hard, but he simply couldn't find her. When her laughter rang around the woods, Liam stilled his steps and looked around. He nearly screamed when she dropped from the tree above him.

"You couldn't find me." His big cat shoved her to the ground. "You have no idea how needy I am. I need to feel his tongue on me. In me, Liam."

Her pants were in shreds when he finally settled down to taste her. She was warm, her cream hot. And when he took his first taste of her, licking her from gate to clit, he moaned while the cat purred. She was theirs and they were going to keep her safe. When she came, screaming out his name, he shifted. Need was pounding at him like it hadn't before.

"I'm breeding, as you call it." He nearly told her she wasn't when she kissed him before continuing. "Mason told me. That's why he didn't take my blood this morning. He said that even you'd not be able to tell yet."

"You were never in heat, not that I know of." She told him that now was not the time to discuss it. "Yes, you're right."

Liam slammed into her. His cock felt strangled when she cried out again and again. And when he started to fuck her, she wrapped her legs around his hips, her arms over his shoulders, and took him with each stroke. Christ, he was going to come, and when he did, he was sure that his head would explode.

Slowing down, just to catch his breath, he held her hands above her head in one of his. She calmed as well. Her legs slid down his and wrapped around his calves. He made love to her then, taking his time to taste her skin, to lick her throat and touch her. When she told him she loved him, he kissed her, taking his time with the kiss as much as she'd let him.

"I will love you forever, Liam. I will never be able to live without you." He kissed her again, holding her face in his hand as he did so. "Take me, please? I need you."

Liam didn't hurry now that he had a second wind. Making love to his wife was nothing like he'd ever experienced before. There was love, yes, and coming together for sure. But the specialness of it, the bond that they were creating, was so much more than two people making love and being in love. It was as if they were finally one, a single entity that could never be taken apart.

He came then, his body simply taking over, and he cried out her name. When Emma bit down on his shoulder, his body came a second time. Not his cock and balls, but his entire body. When he took her hard, making sure that she enjoyed it as much as he had, he bit down on her throat and tasted the difference right away. They were going to have another child.

Holding her while they rested, he thought of the son they

had now, the things they were going to do when the second one came. Liam was so happy that he pulled her tighter against him and kissed her shoulder. Emma looked down at him when he rolled to his back, taking her with him.

"You know it." He nodded. "I don't know what to think about this. It's so.... I was going to say fast, but it's more than that. Exciting and overwhelming. Your parents are going to be over the moon about this."

"They will be. And Edward will have a little brother or sister now." Emma nodded and grinned. "What? What are you thinking?"

"That perhaps we might have twins too. Wouldn't that be a hoot?" He didn't think so, but said nothing. And when she pinched him on the nipple he asked her what that was for. "You aren't excited about having three children all in diapers? I'm not either, but you could have lied to me."

"No, I couldn't have." She lay her head on his chest. "You're the best reason in the world for being alive. And now that I have a child here and one on the way, I don't think I could be any happier."

They made their way to the house and got dressed. Liam was having a hard time not touching her, just running his fingers over her arm. A hand to her back when she walked with him. Making their way to the living room, they were having a discussion about where their children would go to college when Mason walked in. He did look a great deal better than he had earlier. When he sat, his face full of humor, Liam wondered what he was thinking. The man had had a really rough time of it of late.

"I'm better." Emma nodded and asked him if he needed anything. "No, not at the moment. I will go out later, but for now, I'm well. I wanted to tell you about the woman, Willa. It's a long story, if you don't mind."

"No, we don't. I'm glad that you're well." Mason nodded at him. "All right, tell us what happened, then we'll tell you about Burt."

"Very well. She claimed to be my mate." That wasn't a shock. They'd heard that from Rick. "She had all the right cues. In that I mean, she had a scent that called to me. Fresh blood, by the way. I wanted her, which when I think on it, wasn't that difficult to manufacture because of the way she was dressed and appeared. Then there was the simple fact that I think, with all that is going on around here, all the love, I wanted to be in love as well."

"I'm sorry." Mason told him not to be. "So, she wanted you to think all this so that she could get you alone and kill you? She explain to you why?"

"I don't think her plan was to go back to my place with me. I knew what she was about when I touched her hand in mine. But being in the open, where she could shift into anything, would have gotten me killed. I wouldn't have known where she was at any time. At my own home, not only did I know it better, but it was confined as well. I was actually surprised when she agreed to come with me." Liam felt a cold finger of fear run down his back. Christ, she could have been anywhere at any time. "Having her naked, well that had two things going for it, but the most important was that I could see that she was, for the most part, unarmed. I only had to deal with the hair pin. It was made of oak, what would have normally been able to kill a younger vampire, but not one as old as me."

"But you were hurt." Mason nodded at Emma and smiled. "I don't understand then. I'm not sure about vampires and age and what that has to do with wood, either. How were you hurt?"

"I didn't say it wouldn't hurt me. But it can't penetrate my heart. I have...I'm sorry, but I cannot tell you what woods would take my life. Not that I believe you would ever use it against me, but there are beings out there that can read your mind and find it there, and would enjoy taking me to task on things that I have done. Like Willa." Liam asked him if he knew what she'd wanted him dead about. "Oh yes. I murdered her father. Not murdered, I guess, but I did kill him. And it took me a bit to figure out who he might have been when she said that she wanted me to join him in hell. Her dad was a friend of mine. Not a close one, but one that I would consider trustworthy. It turned out, I was wrong in that. He led a group of beings to my lair to kill me. The money, he told me, was too much to pass up."

"Because of things you did to him? Or things that these people thought you might have done?" Mason told him it was the latter. "Did you do these things? And know that you don't have to answer if you don't want to."

"I know that. But I did do some of the things that they thought. However, two of the men thought I had soiled their daughters. It wasn't me. It might have been had they not been...well, it wasn't me." The look on Mason's face made Liam think he thought the idea of having sex with these daughters was too appalling. "I did drink from a few of the men, but they were paid well. A few coins in their pockets would have gone a long way in making sure that I didn't steal from them. And I was taking some liberties with their homes. Sleeping in the barns or a dark basement. Yes, I had done those things. But that didn't warrant them trying to kill me. At least I didn't think so."

CHAPTER 13

The courtroom was filled to standing room only occupancy. Emma looked around for the rest of the Harrisons, and smiled when her aunt led them into the room. The seats where she was sitting filled up just as the room was called to order. Today was going to be a big day for a lot of people.

"Remember what I told you." Emma nodded at her aunt and took her hand in hers. "Don't let him drag you into a heated discussion. Like I said, he's done this all on his own. As much as it pains me to say this, I'm glad that he's getting what he deserves. He is my brother, but he's hurt enough people for far too long."

"He's not going to like either of us very much, I don't think." Aunt Eunice asked her if she cared. "Not really. I mean, deep down I do. It hurts me to think that he did this to us, but he did hurt a lot of people while he was at it."

When her dad was brought out of the side room, she looked at him. He'd aged a bit, she thought. His hair was too long and seemed to have a mind of its own. And the orange and black striped uniform he'd been put in did nothing for his pallor. He was chained at both his ankles and wrists, as well as a collar around his neck that seemed dog-like, but she knew that it was to keep him in line. Her dad wasn't one to take no for an answer, she'd come to realize.

After the judge read off the entire list of things that her father was there for, he asked if he had any questions. Of course, he would, and turned and smiled at her before addressing the judge again.

"I think that there's been a misunderstanding, Your Honor. You see, some of that stuff I didn't do where anyone would have caught me, and the others, well, my daughter, she took care of me for it." The judge looked at the paperwork in front of him while her dad continued. "I did use her house for the loan, and I told her I was sorry for that. But she had told me no when I asked her, and I knew she'd want me to have it anyway, so that's what happened there. As for running off. No, I didn't run off, leaving her with the fallout like you said. I just needed to lay low for a bit until her temper cooled off. It's not a horrible one, but it can make a man feel really bad when he hurts his only child. I knew she'd get over her snit, and that's what I was doing."

"Then perhaps you shouldn't have done it in the first place, if it hurt you so much." Dad nodded, but the judge wasn't finished just yet. "When someone tells you no, Mr. Hudson, do you normally just go ahead and do it anyway?"

"Sure. Sure. It's the way I am. I know that it backfires at times, like this one did, but I mean well. That should count for something. Anyway, I bet if you asked her about it, she'd tell you that she's forgiven me, and then we can take care of the rest of that list you got there." When she was asked to stand, her dad looked at her and smiled. "Hello, darling. You sure do look pretty today."

"Shove it, Dad. Yes, Your Honor, I do wish to press charges against my father for fraud. He forged my name to a loan after I told him no. Several times, as a matter of fact." She looked at her dad then. "You were a rotten person for doing that. I was just starting to get a name for myself, and you screwed that up."

"Now, Hudson—" She told him her name was Emma. "I don't care for your tone, young lady. And you should clear this up for me. I want to be able to spend some time with you and go back out on the road. You tell him you messed up."

She sat down. There wasn't any talking to him when he got like this. And it had only occurred to her recently that he'd been like this all her life. Passive aggressive, Ennis told her. That's what he was using to get what he wanted. And when it didn't go his way, he'd just do it himself and damn the consequences.

"Well, Mr. Hudson, I think that clears that up." Her dad nodded, and she had no doubt that he thought that part of his sentencing was not going to come up again. "What about the rest here? Grand theft? There is also forged log books. You do know that's a no-no, correct?"

"I don't have any forged books. I made sure those were taken care of." He looked at her again when he understood. "You turned over my books to them? Hudson, whatever am I going to do with you? You know better than to do that. Darn it, girl."

"It's against the law to drive over so many hours, you are aware of that, correct?" Dad told the judge that he was, that's why he kept two sets of books. "And that, too, is against the law. But that's water under the bridge when you wrote down that you were at a few places, in fact all the places, that came up with missing merchandise that you were to take to stores."

"I did that. But those companies have no right to make it a big deal, when I know for a fact that they insure that stuff. In case I have an accident or something and ruin all their things. Why don't you just mark those as fixed too? I know you can do it. That's not fair that I get dinged for something they already got paid back for." Her dad looked at her again. "Sure am ashamed of you, Hudson. You did me wrong. When I get back to your house, you got a lot of making up to do before I let you off the hook."

When Liam stood up, she watched her dad. This was his day of reckoning for a great many things. And she was glad to be here when he got it. Not just for her, but for her aunt as well.

"Your Honor, Mr. Hudson threatened my life and that of our newborn son just a few days ago. He told my wife that should she not do as he asked, that he would take care that we were out of the way. Not his exact words, mind you, but close enough. It was brought to my attention that he did this once before. Threatened and killed someone when he didn't get his way." Her dad asked what he was talking about. "Alex Clarke, husband to your sister, Eunice Clarke."

"He was taking up all her time." Her dad looked at the judge. "You have a family. Don't it bother you to no end when they do something without you? She was all the time all over him. And when I came by, she'd not stop once to just talk to me. Besides, that was ruled an accident. I wasn't charged with that one. And I'd make sure I wasn't this time either. He's driving me crazy with all his rules, this one is. And it's not right, Your Honor. She's my daughter. Not to mention, that kid ain't even hers. She went and took somebody else's castoff."

"Castoff? That's just not.... You know, Mr. Hudson, this is only a hearing that is to judge whether or not you should go to trial. A hearing in which people can bring charges against you, in a court of law. You understand that, don't you?" Her dad nodded. "You just self-proclaimed, and without prompting, that you not only stole the merchandise that you were accused of, but forged your daughter's name to loans that you admittedly said she told you no to. Not to mention, you used phony times and pickup information in order to hide the fact that you were not driving according to the letter of the law. Then you self-confessed to not just murdering someone, but that you also threatened two people, one of them a small child. What do you have to say to this?"

"You said that the other matter was taken care of. I know you can do that, just mark it out. Like I said, they got themselves insurance. And I wouldn't have to threaten anybody if someone just paid attention to me when I'm around. This is all Hudson's fault, Your Honor. She's to blame. Give her a big fine...her husband's got all kinds of money. And when he's gone, she and me will have us some fun again. You go on and do that." The judge looked at her when she stood up. "See, she's gonna confess right now."

"Your Honor, he's my father. I know that, but I don't think he's ever going to get that you're telling him that he's been taking advantage of everyone around him since he was a kid. Not just me and my aunt, but the system when it doesn't work for him. Or restaurants when he didn't eat all his meal and demanded half his money back. All my life he's been a bully, using what I've only just realized was passive aggressive forms of abuse on those that dare to try and keep him from what he wants. Even resorting to murder. I would love to say that he'll change now that he's caught, but he's not going to. I want him to pay for his crimes."

"What are you saying, Hudson?" She reminded him again that her name was Emma, Emma Harrison. "I don't care what you're calling yourself. You're my daughter, and I want you to tell this man that you don't want me to go to jail."

"Actually, I do. And the sooner the better, for a lot of people." The judge pounded his gavel down hard when her dad started yelling at her, telling her that it had been a mistake. That she needed to fix this for him. And when he was dragged away, she sat down on the chair hard and felt the world around her tilt and fuzz. Holding her head, she saw the floor coming up at her fast, and found she didn't really care if it hit her or not.

~~~

Liam held her hand while he waited for her to wake. Emma had hit her head pretty hard when she'd fainted, and he was terrified that she would never wake up again. Not really, but there had been so much blood that he'd been out of his mind with terror. His mom sat in the chair across from the bed.

"She's going to be fine. All head wounds bleed a lot." He told her the doctor had said the same thing. "Good. I wanted to talk to you about a couple of things. I'm not doing it because it's something I don't want her to know, but it might distract you a bit, and I think you need that."

"I do. Thanks." She nodded. "Mom, I love her. You know that, but I can't believe how much I love her. It's like my entire world before her was just in a holding pattern until she came to me."

"That's what it's supposed to be like. And I love her as well. She is very special." He nodded. "Now. You can tell me no if you wish, but I would like to buy young Edward things for his room just for him. Computer, printer, and perhaps a desk that fits it all, and anything else he might need as he grows up. I know you can afford it, but I want him to know, all through his life, the circumstances of his birth mean nothing to me."

"Mom, just by doing that, you're singling him out." She said no, she wasn't. "Did you buy the things for the other babies? Their rooms all set up?"

"Yes." That surprised him. "But, officially, he's my very first grandchild. He was born—and I looked into it—he was born a whole eighteen hours before the other two. He's the first, and he gets to be special. With his room, I'm getting him something just from your dad and me, as our first grandchild."

"You've already done it, haven't you?" She nodded and grinned at him. "I should have known. What do the others say about this? Anything that I want to know?"

"Well, they were very upset. Riordan was because he'd not thought of it first. And Darcy said he was going to try and outdo me, so he and Brooke are going to do something I can't, and dedicate a piece in pottery for the little man. Mac said he was going to teach him how to say 'no, Grandma, I have plenty.' I think I dislike him the most right now." He asked what Aedan was going to do. "He's going to let him have a room—well, all the grandchildren—a room at the White House when he is in office. I do hope he can be there, don't you?"

"He will be. He's a Harrison, after all." Mom nodded and said he was right. "I know you know this, but Emma and I are going to have another baby. She's been feeling a little off since Mason told her, but I think now that this thing with her dad is done, she'll be better. And we have a buyer for her rig too. She doesn't want to do that anymore."

"That's wonderful. I have something I'd like for the two of you to do for me. It involves one of the buildings that I own downtown. The next time you go to England, I'd like for you to pick up some things to bring back for me. I want tea cups. A lot of them. I've decided to start having a monthly tea. And if that works out, once a week." He liked that idea and told her he did. "Well, as much as I'd like to take credit, it's Lynn's idea. She said her, her sister, and their mother used to go to one once a month when they were children. I thought that some of the folks at the nursing home would enjoy bringing their daughters and granddaughters. I might even bake a few things."

"I love that idea. But I don't want to go, if it's all the same to you." They both looked at Emma when she spoke. "Hello. I guess I passed out."

"You did. And knocked your noodle good. They want you to lie quietly for a bit longer. And I'll stay with you while Liam goes and gets us both a scone and some tea. Talking about it has given me a craving." Liam kissed Emma on the forehead and then her mouth before asking them what kind. "Black tea for me, and a blueberry scone."

Emma wanted the same and he left them to it. Liam was nearly out of the ER when his cell phone went off. It wasn't a number he recognized, but he answered it in case it was business. Instead it was the jail…Burt was calling him.

"I want to talk to Hudson." He corrected him again. "Why do you care what I call her? Anyway, there's been a mistake. They're not going to let me out of here, pending some trial that she can take care of for me. I can't even get them to let me put one of those ankle things on me so I can take care of business. Tell her to make them."

"No, I won't do that. I think you've done enough damage to her. And we all like you just where you are." Burt started going on like he had in the courtroom earlier. "Did you even want to know if she's all right? You were there when she fell, hitting her head. Did it occur to you to ask about her?"

"Asking about her is not going to clear things up for me here. If she were really hurt, which I think was just a distraction for me to run, I'd be told about it. Tell her the next time she tries something like that to let me know. I could be at her house by now instead of in here." Liam assured him it wasn't anything to do with him. "If you say so. When can I talk to her?"

"You can't. And as soon as we hang up here, I'm calling the jail and asking them to not allow you to bother us again. You're bad news." He said that he couldn't do that to him. "Of course, I can. Emma is my wife and I want her to be healthy. With you around, that's not really possible."

"You're going to regret this, young man. My daughter is all I have. Well, I have a sister too, but she isn't as close to me as Hudson is." Liam corrected him again. "Gosh darn it, I know what her name is. Stop doing that."

"Goodbye, Mr. Hudson. I hope you have a nice life while in prison."

Liam ended the call with him still sputtering around about how Hudson was his daughter. When the call was disconnected, he called the jail and let the man who answered know that Hudson was calling him and threatening him again. The man said he'd take care of it.

Burt would lose his phone privileges, which was a good thing. Nor would he be able to borrow one from anyone that had one on them, if anyone would want to go and see the man. Liam was told that not only would his lawyer, court appointed in his case, know, but so would each shift. It wouldn't happen again. Liam thanked him for that.

After getting the drinks and scones, he made his way back to her room. He met Storm in the hallway as he waited for the elevator. She kissed him on the cheek and asked him what he was doing later.

"Nothing. They're not going to keep Emma, so when she's ready to be released, I'm going to take her home. Why? What did you need?" She asked him if they could come over for dinner. "Sure, if Emma feels like it. What's going on?"

"I have to go out of town for a few weeks." He nodded as the doors closed around them. "Riordan is going with me, and I wanted to know if you could keep an eye on a few things here. Mainly a project I have in the works."

"I can do that for you, you know that." She nodded, but didn't say any more. "Is it a big secret or something?"

"Yes." They entered Emma's area, and he had to wonder if he wanted to help her now. He didn't care for secrets, and hated them more if he couldn't tell Emma about them. Mom was gone when he returned, and he gave Storm her tea and scone. "I have a favor to ask of you both. I would very much like it if you were to keep this under wraps for a few days. When I return, I'll put it out there. But Riordan and I are going to D.C. for a few weeks, and when we come back, everyone will know. Home Cookin is going to go national."

"Wow, that's wonderful." She nodded. "I don't know what to say. That's terrific news. Does Andi know yet?"

"No. I mean, she's sort of been hinted to about it, but I think she's just been too busy. She doesn't cook there much anymore, but it's all her recipes that we use. While in D.C., we're going to have them bound up in a book for her and to share with the other restaurants. I'm so excited, I could bust a nut."

"You don't have a nut to bust, but I get it." Emma sat up more in the bed. "This is amazing. I've never even eaten there yet. I mean, I've been by there and seen the line of people waiting to go in, but I've never had the opportunity to go sit and enjoy the food. I'll have to now."

"You will. But most of the things she cooks, I think you've had. When Mom and Dad have dinner, Andi does most of the planning and cooks a lot of it. It's a stress reliever for her." Liam looked at Storm as he continued. "She's not going to like you much if you throw more on her plate right now. I think she's helping Nikki run Aedan's campaign office as well."

"I know, but I helped them out with that by hiring someone to do most of the work. He's the same guy that Nikki's uncle used to be elected twice. He knows the ropes better than most." That was impressive and much needed, Liam thought. "Also, if you could keep an eye on things around the house, that would be great. We're having some work done on the pool house. I think we're going to have a visitor soon."

"A visitor? Anyone that we might know?" Storm told him that he didn't, but that he was coming in to help with some projects she had going. "Another vet then?"

"Yes, he's been through a great deal, and this is just what he needs, I think. I don't even know a great deal about him other than Howard asked me to put him up for a while. He just lost his wife, and he's taking life in general pretty hard." Liam held onto Emma's hand tighter. He didn't know what he'd do without her. "Anyway, I'll have a complete dossier when I return."

Emma was released a few minutes after Storm left, and he wondered if she had anything to do with that. More than likely, he thought. She could pull more strings than he'd seen in a tree too close to a water hole. Smiling at the thought, as they made their way out of the clinic, Liam wondered what else she needed from them.

Dinner would be wonderful. Just the four of them so they wouldn't have to compete with the others and their voices. He loved his family, more than anything, but they were loud, overbearing, and a bit on the intense side. Spending time with them, all of them, was much like he thought spending time in one of those tornado machines would be. The ones that let you see what it was like to be in all that wind.

Picking up the baby from the nanny, they headed to Storm and Riordan's home. It was set back off the road, and while smaller than his and Emma's was becoming, it was still a massive, impressive pile of bricks. He'd been informed that their house would be completed in a week. Liam couldn't wait. Not just to have the house finished up, but all the workers gone as well. He wanted to be alone with his family at home.

"The pool house is almost finished. But there are a couple of things that we've changed since it was started. A bigger bathroom. Better lighting in the kitchen area. Also, I know this sounds stupid, but we're having another pool house put in, and this one is going to be just that. The original pool house, I'm sure we can use off and on to help someone." Liam agreed with his brother. "This guy that's coming here, I'm sure that Storm told you he's sliding on the downside of depression. He needs to be gotten out when you can. Not all the time, just a little. And check on him. We don't think he'll do anything to himself, but it's hard to tell."

"There are several projects going on in town. Can he get involved with those?" Riordan told Emma that he was confined to a wheelchair. "I'll look into what I can find for him. Involvement does help. And Aunt Eunice can go visit him. It'll be good for her too. She's been down since the pretrial for my dad."

"Thank you. Both of you." Riordan leaned back in his seat as he continued. "We're going to go for a baby soon. I think that we're done doing all this traveling, too. It's been fun, but it's too much when the family needs us. Howard is going to set us up here, with all the bells and whistles, but there will be a great deal less traveling on our end."

"Good. I miss you when you're gone." Riordan said that he missed him as well. "When Aedan is elected, which we're all hoping for, will you help him in the same way?"

"Always."

When they left an hour later, he felt better about things. There were a few more items that he needed to finish up, and a couple more projects that he had to look into. Liam was going to have to go to D.C. himself in a few weeks, but that was only to talk to Howard about some of the items he had him looking into. Housing for when he left the White House in two years. Liam was looking forward to that as well.

CHAPTER 14

Ennis woke up. He was in his office in the chair. Again. This was the third time today that he'd fallen asleep. This time he had a witness to it. Yawning hugely, he asked Mason how long he'd been out.

"Not too long, perhaps twenty minutes or so. You, my friend, are overworked." Ennis agreed with him. "I have a buddy, he's able to come out during the day, who would like to come and join your practice. He doesn't want money, you should know that up front, but he's bored."

"Why work for me?" Mason told him he was a good man. "That's not what I meant and you know it. I mean, why does he want to stave off his boredom by coming to work in this one-horse town?"

"Derick has been a physician for a great many years. He is an excellent surgeon, and has been on the cutting edge of a great many new advances that are practiced today. The last place he was, a hospital setting, was fun for a time, but he hated not getting to know the people that he was helping. Much the same reason that you left your other practice." Ennis rubbed his neck, another sign that he was stressed out. "How long has it been, Ennis, since you had a full night's sleep?"

"I can't remember. And don't get me wrong, I love this. The country doctor making house calls and everything, but I am worn out." He yawned again and rested his head on his hand. He'd be asleep before long, he realized, and put his hand on the desk. "What else should I know about him?"

"His name is Derick Donavan. He's a few hundred years old, I think about seven. No children that he's made, nor any that he's had with a mate. And he did have one, long ago, but she was murdered. There won't be anyone coming for him for the retaliation, but she has been avenged. He's a made vampire rather than a pureblood, which is why he is able to go out during the entire day. He also enjoys a good meal and fine wines." Ennis was ready to tell him to bring him aboard today when Mason continued. "He's here. Now, as a matter of fact. I've been noticing you getting more and more exhausted daily. And while I know that you'd have gotten around to it eventually, Derick approached me about a job and I thought of you."

"Just on your say-so, I'm ready to take him on. But he'd have to be paid. I can't afford to have the income of two doctors and only one of us getting paid for it. I'm assuming that you heard about the bigger place I've been trying to purchase too. I haven't heard—"

"It's yours. I took care of that before coming here." Ennis asked if anyone died. "Good heavens, no. I just put a little suggestion in someone's ear and there it is. You think I'd kill someone for you?"

"Yes. Yes, I do." They both laughed. "All right, I have the building, so I need to order in some supplies. Unless you've done that as well."

"No, I'm afraid that I don't know a great deal about the sort of equipment you'd need, so I'll leave that to you. You do have a nice credit at the wholesale market that deals in that sort of thing. And Derick would like to go with you, to put his two cents worth in, if you don't mind." Ennis said that he didn't. "Good. Then that's settled. I have a house that he is going to take off my hands that isn't far from here. Also, you should think about getting yourself one. That way your parents won't know when you, or in this case when you don't, come home to bed."

"Mom was fussing at me yesterday. Or the day before, I don't remember." Mason said it was three days ago. "She tell you?"

"In a way. I can feel when she's upset. Not at you, but worried, I guess, would have been a better word for it. Your father as well." Ennis nodded. "It's well past lunch. I think you and I should meet your new partner and see what he can do for you. After that, I think a nice long nap is in order."

"What if we don't hit it off?" Mason asked him why he'd think that. "I don't know. I'm so exhausted, I'm not sure where I am half the time."

"Yes, I can see that. You've fallen asleep in your office when I know you have a lovely bed at home. Buy you a home, young Ennis, fill it with things you love, and take yourself a partner. You'll live longer if you do." Nodding, Ennis stood up. "Come now, let's have a nice lunch and you can go home. I've taken the liberty of having your calendar cleared for the day, and your secretary has agreed not to call you unless someone is dying."

He was in the restaurant when he realized that he didn't remember coming here. Ennis hated feeling like this. Making poor decisions was just one of the things that worried him. Another was waking up in the middle of unknown conversations. Ennis looked at the man across from him.

"Derick Donavan. Mason left, saying that you'd wake in a moment." Ennis apologized. "No need for that. You're very overworked. I'd enjoy coming to work with you, help you out as much as you do me."

"I don't have a lot of patients right now. More than I can handle, as you can tell, but it's mostly me that is at fault here. I can't stand to see anyone in pain more than they should be." Derick smiled and ordered for them both when the waitress came. "Thank you. Mason said you were a surgeon as well as a medical doctor."

"I am. Also, I have an OB/GYN after a few other titles. I know that you've been doing some deliveries as well. Good. I don't care when doctors say that they're there for you and skip out on some of what that might entail." Ennis said he'd only delivered one baby so far because he was just starting out. "I heard. Your brother and his wife have adopted him. That's wonderful."

"Edward is thriving now that he's loved and taken care of. What about you? Mason said you have no family around." Derick said that he was much too set in his ways to have someone that hadn't been with him for a long time to try anything new. "You have help then?"

"Yes. A staff that is coming with me. They take care of all the things that I tend to overlook. And when I need them to care for something for me, they can do that as well. Like I was saying, they've been with me for some time."

He and Ennis talked about the job, then moved on to more personal things. Derick liked to fish and cook. He'd traveled a great deal over the years, and was ready to settle down in one place for a change. The house, he found out, was near downtown, but not inside the city limits.

"I've got to find me a place to live. I've been staying with my parents for far too long. I've not been in any kind of hurry, but it's something that I have planned on. Mason has excellent taste in housing." Derick said he loved the one he had now. "I'll have to talk to him about looking for me. It's time, I think."

After having an enjoyable lunch with the man, they settled on when he was going to start. If Mason trusted him, then Ennis would as well. There was something very calming about the man, and he found that he was looking forward to working with him. As he made his way home, he thought of the things he should be doing and realized he just didn't have the energy. Going into the house, he told June, his parents' cook, that he was going to bed, and didn't want to be disturbed.

"Good, sir. Very good. And when you wake, I'll make you a nice fattening meal. You've lost a few of them in the last weeks."

Ennis nodded. He made his way to his room and flopped on his bed. He was out before he thought that he should have undressed.

~~~

Georgie stepped back from the painting she was doing when Derick walked into the room. He didn't walk, but seemed to glide across the floor. She smiled when she realized that his meeting had gone well. She asked him how it had gone.

"Very well. Except for the fact that he kept falling asleep." She was appalled at that and told him that. "No, don't be upset, my dear. He is more overworked than Mason told us. And by his own admission, it's primarily his fault. The man is as nice as any I've ever met before. And his family, Mason tells me, is the same."

"Good. No more working with idiots. I think that last group you worked with was only working for the money. And I know what you're going to say, it makes living much better when you have it, but there is a limit to how much a person can let slide when caring for the ill." She bent over the painting again. "There are some messages for you in your office. I should be finished with this in a few hours."

He didn't point out that she'd told him that yesterday and the day before. Georgie couldn't help it if she was a perfectionist. Painting, she supposed, had been a bad choice when she'd been looking for a hobby all those years ago, but over the decades she'd gotten pretty good. Enough for people to want her art, and she could demand very good coin for them. When she thought she was as done as she could be, she cleaned her brushes and looked it over. To date, this one had taken her the longest to do, but she loved it the most.

The painting was of a field, but it wasn't only that. There were other things in the grass and trees that were just hidden from a glance. She could see the deer with his face peeking out from behind the tree that blended well with his fur. There was a long snake curled around a rock, his skin almost a dead match to it. Georgie looked at the raccoons by the waterfall, the bear just coming out of the tree line. And then there was the great tiger.

Georgie wasn't sure why there was a tiger in this picture. She knew that there weren't any natural to the area she'd seen in her mind when she started on this one. But there he stood, his stripes camouflaging him from the sight of anyone going by him. It was the piercing blue eyes that captured her attention. Almost from the start, it was all she could see when she'd painted this piece.

"It's lovely. You've done a grand job, miss." She smiled at Carl when he handed her a glass of juice, her way of celebrating when she finished a painting. "If you don't mind me saying so, I think this one will sell faster than the Dark Nights one you did."

"I don't know if I want to sell it just yet. I'd like to hang onto it, let it comfort me." He nodded as if he understood her oddities. "Carl, have you heard anything about the Harrison ambush yet?

They're the family that his lordship is going to work for."

"They are said to be a well-loved group. They all, save one, have taken mates. All of them tigers now. A few children are now a part of it as well. They're wealthy, very much so, and very good about their money." She asked him what he meant. "The downtown area is thriving, mostly due to them. One of the men is governor of the state, and he is making great strides in getting more jobs in the area, as well as the rest of them revitalizing the area. School expansions as well as updates. New computers in the employment offices. There is a restaurant that caters mostly to the homeless and vets. I believe that a great many of them work there, putting something down on their resume so that they can find employment. A doctor, as you know, as well as an artist. Potter. I think you know the work. Rickson, Brooke Rickson."

"Yes, I knew the elder. He passed away some time ago. His daughter—" Carl corrected her. "His granddaughter is quite good as well, I'm to understand."

"Some say better than the elder." Carl told her that if they had skeletons in their closet, then he couldn't find them. "Also, you might be interested to know that one of the mates is related to the president. Uncle to niece, I believe."

When he left her, she finished cleaning her room up. The studio had been her saving grace over the years. The only thing, at times, that kept her from begging Derick to release her from their bond. She would have killed herself when he allowed it, if he allowed it, but she was better now. Closing up the room, she hoped that she'd be able to come back and work later, but she had things to prepare for before they left for the new house.

Derick was just putting the phone in the cradle when she entered his office.

"You are going to love me." She told him that she already

did. "Be that as it may, but I have purchased you a building. One that you will be able to use as an art room. And there is plenty of space for you to have a gallery, as you've wished, on the lower floor."

"Really?" He nodded and smiled at her. "I have my own studio and rooms? Really? Thank you so much, Derick. Thank you."

"You're very welcome. And if you're close to being finished with your latest work, I can have everything moved in before we leave here." She said she was done. "Good. The moving crew will come in and pack you up, and then you'll be at the other end before me. I start working with Ennis on Monday. That gives us four days to get settled."

"Everything that you wanted to take is packed. The furniture is in the moving vans and on its way. And the cars are staying here. For now, you said." He nodded. Derick had quite a collection of cars. "I have my own studio."

"Yes, you do. And now, if it's all right with you, I'm going to go out for a bit. I'll be returning by nightfall. Don't wait up if I'm late. I know you will, but I can still say it."

By the time the crew showed up to pack her things, she had a lot of it in boxes. The pictures were loaded first, with the exception of the one that she'd just finished. Within two hours she was not only on her way with her own load of things, but she was rearranging things in her mind. Not that she'd seen the rooms yet, but she wanted to set it up perfectly. Georgie was nearly shaking with delight.

Before You Go...

HELP AN AUTHOR

write a review

THANK YOU!

Share your voice and help guide other readers to these wonderful books. Even if it's only a line or two your reviews help readers discover the author's books so they can continue creating stories that you'll love. Login to your favorite retailer and leave a review. Thank you.

AWARD WINNING, BESTSELLING AUTHOR

Kathi Barton, winner of the Pinnacle Book Achievement award as well as a best-selling author on Amazon and All Romance books, lives in Nashport, Ohio with her husband Paul. When not creating new worlds and romance, Kathi and her husband enjoy camping and going to auctions. She can also be seen at county fairs with her husband who is an artist and potter.

Her muse, a cross between Jimmy Stewart and Hugh Jackman, brings her stories to life for her readers in a way that has them coming back time and again for more. Her favorite genre is paranormal romance with a great deal of spice. You can visit Kathi online and drop her an email if you'd like. She loves hearing from her fans. aaronskiss@gmail.com.

Follow Kathi on her blog: http://kathisbartonauthor.blogspot.com/